THE DOCTOR WHO FILE

DATE DUE

LUCINDA KITZELMANN

THE DOCTOR WHO FILE
PETER HAINING

W.H. ALLEN · LONDON
1986

This File is for
all the Doctor's fans:
in the past-time
the present-time
and the future-time

Copyright © Peter Haining, 1986
'Doctor Who' series copyright © British Broadcasting
Corporation, 1986
This book is published by arrangement with the British
Broadcasting Corporation

Typeset by Phoenix Photosetting, Chatham, Kent
Printed and bound in Great Britain by
Mackays of Chatham Ltd, Chatham, Kent
for the Publishers, W. H. Allen & Co. Plc
44 Hill Street, London W1X 8LB

British Library Cataloguing in Publication Data

Haining, Peter
    The Doctor Who file.
    1. Doctor Who (Television programme)
    I. Title
    791.45 72   PN1992.77.D6/

ISBN 0–491–03813–5

CONTENTS

MARK BENTHAM

THE AUTOMATIC LOG: AN INTRODUCTION

THERE IS surely no more wonderful creation in the many worlds of *Doctor Who* than the TARDIS, the Doctor's transdimensional machine, bigger on the inside than out, that has carried him – and us, his admiring audience – to the most fabulous places and times. Into situations of peril and excitement, and even face-to-face encounters with monsters and alien beings beyond our wildest imaginings.

Over the years, the six regenerations of the Doctor have – story by story, and piece by intriguing piece – let us into some of the secrets of this machine: the name of which is actually an acronym for Time And Relative Dimensions In Space. We have learned quite a lot about the console which governs its flights, a little about the array of rooms and equipment that lie beyond the walls of the control room, and even just a hint of its awesome powers.

At the heart of the TARDIS, we know, lies the vastly complex Memory Computer in which is stored all the accumulated information necessary for its smooth – if sometimes erratic – functioning. Linked to this is the Automatic Log which records all the data concerning the ship's journeys – data which the Doctor can recall for information or apply to guide the machine by the simple use of the two sets of switches on Console Panel Five. The right hand set of these

Below: The first Doctor as played by the late William Hartnell;
Opposite: The control console, storehouse of all the TARDIS data

is used to automatically direct the ship, while the other, on the left, is for the collection and assimilation of information.

That second panel has excited my imagination ever since I learned the Doctor could use it audio-visually for adding information: both from his own experiences and with whatever he might have gathered from others – human, alien or even machine! And after twenty-three years of travel from one end of time and space to the other, just *think* what stories and secrets lie there awaiting disclosure . . .

I am sure, too, because of the Doctor's unique power of foresight that he has had the good sense to store in the Automatic Log all the thoughts and impressions of those who have been intimately associated with him in making the programme about his adventures such an international success. Some, I suspect, are too secret to be revealed, while others perhaps a little too personal!

I have, nevertheless, through a little

ingenuity, a lot of perseverence, and with the approval of the Time Lords (BBC branch, that is), been able to tap into the Automatic Log for long enough to retrieve the recollections of a representative group of people intimately associated with each of the six regenerations of the Doctor. They range from producers to script editors, and from monster makers to the actual actors who have played the Doctor.

There are, though, no recollections from any of our Time Lord's numerous companions, nor from his arch-enemy, the Master. The Automatic Log makes it clear that in the case of his travelling companions, *their* memories are considered rather too imprecise and emotional to be objective (and the Doctors have, as a general rule, of course, preferred they keep their thoughts to themselves, anyway!); while the Master's recollections are recorded as being *much* too inspired by evil intentions to be trustworthy! There is, though, one exception to this rule: Tom Baker's redoubtable friend, Ian Marter, who just happens to be the only suitable person to let us in on the secret of what should have been the great *Doctor Who* movie . . .

The Doctor Who File is, I must admit, far from complete. So much more undoubtedly resides in the TARDIS Memory Banks and only time – the Doctor's time – will allow us further

opportunities to tap its fabulous knowledge. For the time being, though, here are a kaleidoscope of memories from the history of the greatest television hero of them all . . .

Peter Haining
Earth Date: December 1985.

P. CRAWLEY

BARRY PIGGOTT

THE DOCTOR'S FILE

Section One: Extract from The Daily Mirror *Date 1980.*
Subject: Doctor Who
Born: 1075 on the planet Gallifrey, in the Constellation of
Kasterborous (first seen on TV in 1963).
Background: Doctor of Science. Renegade from the Time
Lords, the leaders of Gallifrey, who monitor happenings in
Time and Space. They are concerned with the Doctor's
interference in the affairs of other races and occasionally
interfere.
Distinguishing Characteristics: Assumes a new body when the
old one shows signs of ravage. (Hence, the various Doctor
Whos.) Flamboyant, though often eccentric dresser. Also has
two hearts.
Motivation: Greatest do-gooder of our time.
Hobby: Toys with electronics.
Matrimonial Status: Unknown. Little time or inclination for sex
or emotion. Eye for attractive and rather young girls.

Section Two: Extract from Official BBC File. Date Present Day.
Subject: Who is *Doctor Who*?
Just about the most popular character on British television. For

twenty-three years now, the mysterious Time Lord who bears this name has been shuttling through time and space, sorting out galactic problems and vanquishing monsters and alien enemies, to the immense delight of a multi-million audience.

The Doctor is a national institution; an outstanding character of modern fiction whose charismatic quality has triggered off one of the biggest merchandising packages associated with a British TV programme; as well as dozens of active fan clubs around the world.

Thirty-eight countries share the British enthusiasm for the *Doctor Who* television series.

The Doctor is a Time Lord, the possessor of two hearts, a body temperature of 60 degrees fahrenheit and immense longevity. Bored with Gallifrey – his own super-advanced planet – and his fellow Time Lords, he roams through space and time in a personalised ship – the TARDIS (Time And Relative Dimensions In Space).

In practice, his spaceship is temperamental and unreliable. The Chameleon Circuit having jammed on a visit to London in the Sixties left the TARDIS's exterior as a police box.

Nor is the Doctor himself infallible. Part of his appeal is his problem-solving capacity when things go wrong, making do through his own ingenuity or with whatever electronic gadgetry that happens to be around.

The Doctor has the ability to regenerate into a new body; to date there have been six Doctors, each very different, played by William Hartnell, Patrick Troughton, Jon Pertwee, Tom Baker, Peter Davison and currently, Colin Baker.

Doctor Who is not a children's programme – it appeals to all age groups and to people from all walks of life. It is a fantasy programme of good against evil – a departure into fun and adventure . . .

BARB ARMATA

WHO WAS SYDNEY NEWMAN?

JOHN LUCAROTTI, a leading television script writer, has for many years been a close friend of Sydney Newman, the man who dreamed up the idea of Doctor Who. John had previously worked as script editor on Newman's ABC series, The Avengers, and was one of the first writers to be contacted when the ebullient Canadian moved to the BBC and began making the series about an eccentric time-traveller which he had first — unsuccessfully — tried to launch at ABC. In the following essay, John writes about his association with Sydney Newman and also of his own pioneer contributions to the series, 'Marco Polo' (1964), 'The Aztecs' (1964) and 'The Massacre' (1966). Like the Doctor, John Lucarotti is something of a wanderer and now lives on the delightfully unspoiled island of Corsica, where, apart from writing, he also runs with his wife a restaurant called 'Phileas Fogg', named after Jules Verne's intrepid round-the-world traveller. Sydney Newman, too, has left Britain and returned to his native Canada where he is now a senior official on the National Film Board of Canada.

MY INTRODUCTION to *Doctor Who* took place more than a decade before its inception. I was a copywriter in a Toronto advertising agency when I met Sydney Newman, the Head of Drama for the Canadian Broadcasting Corporation. He was, and still is, an admirable man, a brash, enthusiastic and honest showman with a razor-sharp critical sense and a cameraman's eye. He produced my first television play directed, incidentally, by one of his protégés, Arthur Hiller, of *Love Story* fame and other successful films.

Then Sydney crossed the Atlantic to become the Head of Drama for ABC Television (now Thames). I followed about six months later and he employed me as a story editor on a series he had developed. It was called *The Avengers*. But I was not a good company man and resigned three months later to freelance as a writer. He accepted my idea for a seven-part serial entitled *City Beneath The Sea* and I was with him in his office as he read the first script. Suddenly, he threw it on his desk.

'What kinda rubbish is this, Johnny?' he shouted.

'Wait till you meet the villain, Sydney,' I replied, 'he's just like you.' Sydney roared with laughter and there were no more criticisms.

The BBC captured his services as Head of Drama whilst I was living in Majorca where I received a letter from the late David Whitaker asking me if I would be interested in contributing to a new series Sydney had set up with Verity Lambert as Producer (he had abducted her from ABC) and David as Story Editor.

I flew to London, was told the format and that Terry Nation was currently writing a serial set in the future with strange 'robots' called the Daleks.

'Where do you want to go?' Verity asked.

'Into the past,' I replied.

'We've done a Stone Age one,' David remarked, 'what have you in mind?'

Nothing, I thought, and then I remembered that I had written a fifteen-part, half-hour radio serial in Canada during 1956 about the three journeys of Marco Polo and, seven years on, I still had my notes and a copy of his diary.

'Marco Polo,' I said bravely. Verity and David exchanged a glance.

'You're on,' Verity said. David remarked that

Above: Sydney Newman, the man responsible for Doctor Who;
Opposite: Susan (Carole Ann Ford), Barbara (Jacqueline Hill) and Ian (William Russell) in John Lucarotti's story, 'Marco Polo'

if it were a seven-parter, combined with Terry Nation's next six-parter 'The Keys of Marinus', it would complete the second batch of thirteen stories. 'Seven, it is,' Verity replied and the meeting was over.

David had asked for detailed storylines before I wrote the actual scripts but, back in Majorca, I found that by the fourth I was bogged down. I didn't know my characters. Not even the Doctor. I needed to write scenes to discover them. I spent four hours in the local village post-office trying to telephone David at the Beeb to explain my hang-up. When, finally, I spoke to him on an appalling line he simply said, 'Do it your way.'

Which is what I did.

By the time the seventh script was delivered I was back living in London. Verity had chosen the talented Waris Hussein to direct the serial (his second, the other being 'An Unearthly Child' which launched the whole show). His casting was brilliant. Apart from the regulars – Bill Hartnell, William Russell, Jacqueline Hill and Carole Ann Ford – Waris chose Mark Eden as Marco Polo, Derrin Nesbitt as Tegana and the lovely, nineteen year-old Zienia Merton as Ping-Cho who stopped the show when she recorded *The Tale of The Hashashins* in one take. At the end, everyone on the studio floor and in the booth applauded her.

There was also a superb character actor named Martin Miller who played Kublai Khan, but the characterisation was not my invention. In the original radio version I had written him as 'the mighty Khan' but the director had the actor play the role completely against the lines and he became a fussy, endearing little administrator ('Uncle Jenghez was the warrior in the family') with a domineering wife. For 'Marco Polo' he was written as the latter and Martin and Bill had a wonderful 'anything you can do I can better' relationship. It was sheer joy to watch them out-acting each other.

For me, Bill hit his stride in 'Marco Polo'. He was a dedicated, diligent actor and in the previous serials I formed the impression that he was seeking the Doctor's identity. He was Doctor Who, the star of the series, but the first

story, set in the Stone Age, was a 'shake-down' for all the regulars; in the second, Terry Nation's Daleks stole the show and in the third the action was limited to the TARDIS. But in 'Marco Polo' Bill found his direction and crystallised his performance with the authority and stature he brought to it for the next three years.

'Marco Polo' was a very happy programme and Waris had a marvellous group of technicians working with him. One burly red-haired cameraman would interrupt studio rehearsals to say 'hang on a mo', guv, I can get a better shot by doing this,' and then repositioning his camera to achieve the impossible. Waris never argued. The serial was recorded at the BBC's Lime Grove Studios with filmed inserts shot at Ealing.

'The Aztecs' followed on rapidly. In fact, I was writing the scripts whilst 'Marco Polo' was being recorded. Once again Verity and David had given me my head and I had always been intrigued by a race that could be, at the same time, so cultivated and so barbarous. The Aztecs

calculated the length of a year to a decimal point of a second but they never knew about the wheel. The Spaniards, led by Cortez, defeated the Aztecs because on the eve of the final battle fifteen thousand hearts from the élite of the Aztec army were cut out to implore their God, Huitzilipochtli, to bring them victory!

To my mind 'The Aztecs' was a more complex serial than 'Marco Polo' as it dealt in far greater depth with the human relationships and conflicts of those involved. Essentially, it was Barbara's show as she was the central character, the reincarnation of an Aztec God, but then again both Ian and Susan had to contend with their personal difficulties; Ian with Ixta, the chosen leader of the Aztec warriors (a very impressive performance by Ian Cullen) and Susan betrothed to the Perfect Victim. John Ringham's personification of evil as the High Priest of Sacrifice, Tlotoxl, was a masterly contrast to Keith Pyot's Autloc, the High Priest of Knowledge. In one sense Bill took a back seat in 'The Aztecs', although, at the end he found the way for them to return to the TARDIS in the tomb. And his Quixotic 'romance', for devious reasons, with Cameca, beautifully played by Margot van der Burgh, in the Garden of the Elders was a consummate delight to watch.

I enjoyed 'Marco Polo' enormously but I loved 'The Aztecs', which was excellently directed by John Crockett and brilliantly designed by Barry Newbery.

Alas, 'The Massacre' was another story. It was written almost two years after 'The Aztecs'. Both Verity and David had moved on to other shows and the new producer, John Wiles, as well as his story editor, the late Donald Tosh, and I did not see eye-to-eye. To begin with, the subject matter of the St. Bartholomew's Day Massacre of 1572 in Paris was imposed on me and the absence of Bill as the Doctor seemed to me incongruous, even if he did appear as the Abbot of Amboise, an ecclesiastical *Doppelgänger*.

The director, Paddy Russell, did the best she could with what I considered a botched-up idea with frequent inconsistent rewriting and a dénouement I thought ridiculous. Hopefully, where the television version failed, the novelisation will succeed.

We can all be wise after the event but looking back over twenty years ago to the early days of Doctor Who, four names come immediately to mind. Verity Lambert who nursed the series into life, David Whitaker who extracted the best from his writers, William 'Bill' Hartnell who breathed life into the Doctor and, juggling the strings in the background, that cocksure little Canadian, Sydney Newman, who had created the most successful, longest-running science-fiction programme in television history.

Opposite: The evil Tlotoxyl (John Ringham) orders the slaying of the Perfect Victim in 'The Aztecs'

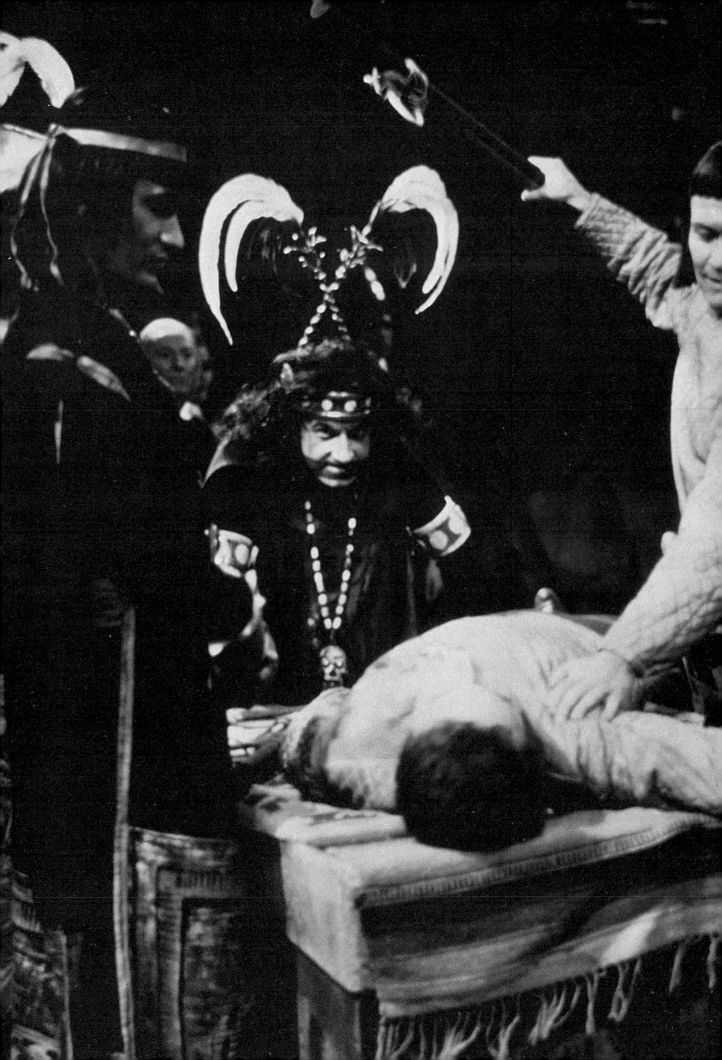

THE MAN
WHO PUT SCIENCE
INTO 'DOCTOR WHO'

VERITY LAMBERT, the first producer of Doctor Who, *is today one of the most important figures in the film industry, and frequently described in the press as, 'Britain's first lady movie mogul.'* Doctor Who *provided her with the first step up the ladder to this dizzy height, and she remains enthusiastic about the programme as well as grateful to Sydney Newman who gave her the chance to launch the series in 1963. Fame came quickly and a major* Daily Mail *feature on her just a year later in November 1964 was headlined, 'Behind Every Dalek There's This Woman'. Here, though, Verity recalls the two men who were behind her in setting up the programme, in particular Mervyn Pinfield, the man who 'put science into* Doctor Who'. *Apart from serving as Associate Producer from 1963 to 1965, Mervyn also directed two stories, 'The Senorites' (1964) and 'Planet of Giants' which opened the programme's second season in the autumn of 1964 and proved the infant show was now a healthy and rapidly growing child . . .*

AN UNSUNG hero in the early success of *Doctor Who* was undoubtedly Mervyn Pinfield who was our Associate Producer. He was appointed to be Technical Adviser to myself and Story Editor, David Whitaker, because, quite simply, neither of us actually knew very much about science!

There we were, running a new programme which was scientific in essence, and also with a brief from Sydney Newman to 'use television'. That is to say, to make full use of all the medium's resources and new developments in order to give it an authentic look. Our aim, we were told, was to expose children to science and history and hopefully interest them in it.

The help that Mervyn was able to give us was absolutely vital. He loved science and he loved television, and he was always abreast with every new development.

We were very nervous making our first few serials, I remember, simply because we were doing things that had rarely been done before – and certainly not by the BBC. As a result, David and I relied heavily on Mervyn to read through all the story ideas and see if they could be done easily and within our budget. If he found problems, he would invariably suggest ways of modifying them so that they could be done with photographic tricks.

One of his earliest contributions was the opening graphics of *Doctor Who*. He devised that innovative sequence of swirling electronic patterns to convey a feeling of travelling in time.

The sequence was actually accomplished by having a television camera filming its own monitor screen. The electronic feedback thus created was allowed to 'bleed' by shifting the image slightly, and a recording was made. From edited segments of this the title graphics were made. Today, the process is familiarly known as a 'signal howlaround'.

Our budget for the show was £2,500 per episode and this meant that we had to rely

Verity Lambert (centre) and the cast of Doctor Who celebrating the programme's first anniversary

heavily on people being highly inventive and doing their best with what little money we could give them.

Building the TARDIS, for instance, was an enormous initial outlay because everything about the huge interior had to be quite new and different. There was nothing we could use from stock. Here again Mervyn came up with some ingenious ideas.

The now familiar six-sided control console consumed much time, effort and expense as the designers worked on all the flashing lights, instruments and dials, not to mention the central column – the time rotor – which not only had to rise and fall, but rotate internally as well!

It was possible, of course, for us to save some of our budget by doing historical dramas among the science stories and using costumes from stock. But this still did not prevent us running into a crisis which very nearly killed off *Doctor Who* before it had hardly begun its scheduled year-long season.

When I joined the BBC, Sydney Newman had been busy transforming the Corporation in the light of what the new commercial networks were doing. He had all but closed down the Children's Television Department, and programmes which normally would have been handled by this Department – like *Doctor Who* – were put under the Drama Department.

This naturally led to some ill-feeling between the two Departments. A lot of people assumed because of what we were spending on the 'science' stories that we were using up considerable sums of money at the expense of the Children's Department. They couldn't, or wouldn't, see how we could spread the costs. Sydney Newman and Donald Wilson were constantly having to refute the attacks upon us.

Ironically, it was the Daleks which brought matters to a crisis point. It began when Donald Wilson first saw Terry Nation's scripts for 'The Daleks'. Having spent so much time defending *Doctor Who* because he believed in it, he saw the Daleks as bug-eyed monsters which went against what he felt should be the theme of the science-fiction stories.

There was strong disagreement between us as a result, and David, Mervyn and I had to argue strongly for the Daleks. Donald, though, was adamant and told us not to do the show.

What saved it in the end was purely the fact that we had nothing to replace it in the time allotted! It was the Daleks or nothing!

The rest, of course, is history, and once the Daleks had rocketed us into the ratings, the friction between the Departments disappeared. Donald Wilson also came and told me, 'You obviously understand this programme better than I do. I'll leave it to you.'

On reflection, I think the success of the Daleks was due to their shape and voices. They are evil but at the same time, they're pitiful as well. In a way they're like huge adult toys!

Mervyn and David were also very supportive of the strong view I had right from the start about the level of intelligence we were aiming at. Although *Doctor Who* was going out at a time when there was a large audience of children, it was intended more as a story for the whole family.

In any case, children then, as now, are very sophisticated, and I was all against scripts which seemed to talk down to them. They are prepared to suspend their disbelief, but they are also very tough and will see through you if you try to patronise them.

The story of the casting of Bill Hartnell as the Doctor is also just as well known as that of the Daleks. But we did have other considerations. David Whitaker was a strong advocate for Cyril Cusack, while Mervyn liked the idea of that other veteran actor, Leslie French, playing the part. How different things might have been if either of those two splendid characters had been cast can now only be a matter for conjecture!

Looking back at the series since my departure, I think Tom Baker's Doctor has been the most faithful to the ideal laid down in the original concept back in 1963. Patrick Troughton was a little whimsical, while Jon Pertwee's Doctor, as virtually an employee of the establishment organisation, UNIT, was a very radical departure from the mould. Peter Davidson had something of Bill Hartnell in his interpretation of the Doctor, while the latest arrival, Colin Baker, also shows something of his character in moments of stubbornness.

I have fond memories of my years with *Doctor Who* – and in particular those two splendid men with whom I worked, David Whitaker and Mervyn Pinfield. It is tragic that they are both no longer with us to see what has become of their visionary work.

FOR LOVE OF THE DOCTOR

HEATHER HARTNELL *knew the first Doctor better than anyone – for she was his wife and constant source of encouragement to him as he created the character of the time-traveller and then made him a huge success. A former actress, Heather became a writer as her husband's career developed, and shared in both his moments of triumph as well as in his later sad ill-health and death in 1975. After the publication of my first* Doctor Who *book,* A Celebration, *which I dedicated to the memory of William Hartnell, Heather wrote thanking me for this gesture which, she said, 'left not a dry eye in the family.' She also offered to tell me her own more intimate memories of her husband as the Doctor 'for when you write Volume Two of the story – which I am sure you will do.' She was right, of course, just as her husband had been in his belief in the idea of* Doctor Who, *and from several conversations with her I compiled the following essay written, precisely as the title suggests, 'For Love Of The Doctor'. My only regret is that Heather, who died in December 1984, will not be able to see this tribute in print – for it is as much a tribute to her as to the man who helped make* Doctor Who *an international institution . . .*

CURIOUS AS IT may seem, the twist of fate which presented Bill with the opportunity of creating the role of *Doctor Who* occurred during the run of that famous London play, *Seagulls Over Sorrento*, in the Fifties. He had signed up for the duration of the play, expecting it to run for weeks whereas, of course, it became a smash hit and lasted four years.

During the course of this run, our daughter, Judith, met and fell in love with the man who was to become her future husband, an agent named Terry Carney. Although we had no way of knowing it then, he was to play an important part in the casting of *Doctor Who*. So you might say that the success of the Doctor is all due to a love match!

William Hartnell as he appeared in the tenth anniversary production 'The Three Doctors'

After the show finished, Bill went into television and created another role for which he is still remembered, that of the bawling Sergeant Major Bullimore in *The Army Game*. Though it made him a household name, it also got him firmly typecast as a 'heavy' and, as you know, he played a whole string of parts as sergeants, detectives, prison officers and crooks. I sometimes think this was a shame, because early in his career Bill had toured with a whole series of comedies, and he was an absolute master at dead-pan comedy which I think is the funniest kind of all.

In any event, by the early Sixties, when Bill was over fifty, he decided he had had enough playing tough parts. By this time, Terry, our son-in-law, was his agent, and Bill told him, 'Try and get me some character parts. It doesn't matter how small they are so long as they give me the chance to become a character actor.'

The chance came soon after this conversation when they were casting for the Richard Harris film, *This Sporting Life*, and were looking for someone to play the rather pathetic old rugby scout. Bill seized the opportunity and, of course, made a tremendous success of it. As a direct result he was offered *Doctor Who* – and I shall never forget the day it happened.

We were living at Mayfield in Sussex then, and Terry phoned from London saying that he was coming down immediately. He had received this incredible script that he wanted Bill to read.

'What's it about?' I naturally asked.

'Well,' he replied a little hesitantly, 'it's actually a children's serial.'

Immediately I could sense what Bill's reaction would be. On the other end of the phone, Terry knew what I was thinking.

'I don't know what he is going to say,' he said, 'but I really believe he should look at it.'

'It's not a tough guy part, is it?' I asked warily.

'No, no,' he said instantly. 'It's an old man with long white hair, an old professor who is a bit round the bend!'

What a marvellous first description of the now world-famous time traveller! Anyhow, I thought from what Terry said that Bill *would* love the part, and so later that day he turned up with the script.

Everything went quiet in the cottage as Bill sat in his chair reading the script from beginning to end. As he closed the last page, he looked up and grinned at us both.

'My goodness!' he enthused. 'I want this part.'

On reflection I can see that Bill knew immediately that there was something so different about the whole idea, and he never had a moment's doubt that it was right for him. In hindsight, too, the only thing I am sorry about was that from the beginning of *Doctor Who* they made him into this rather grumpy old man.

You will remember how he got furious with the school master and mistress who discovered the TARDIS and got into it, and how he took them off on the very first trip really out of spite! I know Bill would have liked to have put more comedy into the part, and to a degree he did try with those exasperated little coughs and splutters.

Even so, he loved the part and had absolute faith in the show even when others expressed doubts that it would last more than a few weeks. The whole *Who* company were a very happy group, and I think that was what made it such a success. They all thought the idea was wonderful and it came through in their acting.

Bill put a lot of himself into the part, of course, and being the kind of person he was, didn't suffer fools gladly. This came out very strongly in the character of the Doctor, and also on the set. I remember he once said, 'Sometimes I have to put my foot down with a new director and tell him, "I *know* how to play Doctor Who and I don't want you to intrude on it or alter it."'

Bill knew that he could get irritated with people – including me! I remember he confessed to a newspaper journalist after the show had become a success, '*Doctor Who* has given me a certain neurosis and it's not easy for my wife to cope with. I get a little agitated, and it makes me a little irritable with people.'

It was not hard to forgive him, though, because he was always absolutely marvellous with children who were the ones, after all, that the show was first intended for.

Bill adored children, in fact, and I think he should have had a family of about six instead of just one daughter. He had a special way with children and spoke to them on their own level. He never, ever, talked down to them, and they respected him for it.

ROBERT SMITH

S. C. Le Vesconte

S. C. LE VESCONTE

Whenever he used to come home to Sussex after filming in London, either when he got off the train or walked to the local shops, there would always be twenty or thirty children to welcome him and follow him around. It was almost as if he was the Pied Piper!

Those children really got to know his habits, and he never got tired of them following him. Do you know they even used to follow us both when we went down to the pub for a drink – and wait outside until we came out!

Bill saw himself as a kind of cross between the Wizard of Oz and Father Christmas – a personality who could hypnotise children.

'Although I portray a mixed-up old man, I have discovered I can hypnotise children,' he told the columnist Matt White in 1965. 'Hypnosis goes with the fear of the unknown. I communicate fear to children because they don't know where I'm going to lead them. This frightens them and is the attraction of the series.'

The first Doctor (William Hartnell) explains the workings of Dalek technology to the Thals in 'The Daleks'

Patrick Troughton as the second Doctor; 'just imagine the Doctor as a Yeti or a Cyberman!'

Fifteen years after 'The Invasion' the second Doctor and the Brigadier (Nicholas Courtney) are reunited in 'The Five Doctors'

The dandy and the clown: the third Doctor (Jon Pertwee) and his predecessor in the tenth anniversary story 'The Three Doctors'

The Doctor in his colourful roadster 'Bessie' which sported the number plate WHO 1!

As the part of the Doctor developed, Bill was always trying to expand it and add new fragments here and there. He had plenty of freedom to improve and build on the original concept, and undoubtedly created a magical figure still widely remembered.

Bill also proposed a number of the *Doctor Who* stories, and though he liked doing many of them, I think the historical tales were perhaps his favourites.

As far as individual stories are concerned, I remember there was a bit of trouble over the first Dalek adventure. The script called for one of the Daleks to be wrecked and for a lot of blood-like ooze to come out of its base. Bill was horrified.

'That must go,' he insisted. 'It is too nasty for children.'

And so the scene was cut. Bill loved the Daleks, though – they were something for him to hate and he knew that the children enjoyed them, too.

He would dearly have loved to play the Doctor in the two full-length Dalek films made with Peter Cushing, but he just didn't have the time. The programme was then on for forty-eight weeks of the year, and when his four weeks of holiday came he certainly needed the break.

Despite his work schedule, Bill would always try and find time to make personal appearances. He was always being inundated with requests to open fêtes, bazaars, even new shops. He was even invited to give away school prizes! He never asked for a fee, though if he was given anything he would always donate it to his favourite charity, Guide Dogs For The Blind.

My most enduring memory of this kind was in 1965 when he opened the big annual fête at Pembury Hospital in Kent. A friend of Bill's had a beautiful old 1903 De Dion Bouton open touring car, and he used this to drive him to the fête.

The car had met Bill and myself in Tunbridge Wells where he had changed into his complete *Doctor Who* costume with wig, cape and stick. Bill sat in the front with me in the back and we set off for the hospital. Well, by the time we had only gone a few miles, there was a whole cavalcade of children and cars and bicycles following us!

It was a fantastic sight – and by the time we reached the hospital the whole place went mad. I shall never forget Bill's face as he gazed at that sea of young children staring at him. And amongst them were our own two grandchildren, Judith and Paul, just as enthralled as all the rest. It was pure magic!

It was ill health, of course, that forced Bill to leave the show, and it broke his heart. Having told everyone that *Doctor Who* was going to run for five years he was determined to see that it did.

Towards the end, though, he found it very hard going, and between 1966 and when he made 'The Three Doctors' in 1972, he got progressively weaker mentally and physically. He could not remember his lines and his legs would give way under him from time to time. That is the awful thing about arteriosclerosis, because as the arteries close up the flow of blood is not only weakened to the limbs but to the brain as well.

It was a terrible trial for him to make 'The Three Doctors' because he couldn't remember a single line. But everyone was very good and for a time he glowed again as if it had taken ten years off his illness.

He was also delighted when Patrick Troughton took over the show, because Bill had actually suggested him for the part. We had both known Pat for years, and he is a marvellous person. Bill was pleased with Pat's interpretation of the part, but after a time he stopped watching because it upset him emotionally that he was not there. He hardly saw any of Jon Pertwee's stories before his death, but I know that to the end he was tickled pink to think that what he had started had lasted for so long. For myself I was also so pleased that more or less the last acting role that he was able to do should be something that has proved so enduring.

I was also delighted that *Doctor Who* got him away from the 'heavy' roles. You have to remember that when you are playing the same part day in and day out, it begins to rub off. When he was playing the Doctor he was delightful to live with because he was so happy.

If Bill had one regret from his time as Doctor Who it was that the programme was in black and white. Because, you see, all the costumes were so colourful, and like all actors he loved dressing up. It just seemed such a shame to him that the viewers couldn't see all those wonderful sets and costumes in all their glory!

'THE SON OF DOCTOR WHO'

The first Doctor meets the mighty Kublai Khan
(Martin Miller) in 'Marco Polo'

THE NEWS THAT the part of Doctor Who is to be played by a new actor comes as no real surprise to me. For I believe that I had something to do with the idea of the Doctor getting another body.

You see, back in 1964 I proposed something along these lines to the executives at the BBC. My suggestion was that the Doctor should have a son, and the new programme could therefore be called, *The Son of Doctor Who*.

The idea, basically, was that this son would be a wicked person. We would both look alike and have our own TARDIS machines to travel in outer space and time. It would have meant, of course, that I would have to play a dual role whenever I 'met' with him, but then the marvels of modern television can make anything possible!

However, the BBC didn't find this idea acceptable, and so I forgot all about it very quickly. But I still think it would have worked and been exciting to children.

It is not many people who are fortunate enough to have the ideas which have a profound

effect upon a programme – nor, indeed, be able to turn them into a workable script – but I do think that something of the idea of the Doctor being able to regenerate into a new body came about as a result of my original suggestion.

People may be surprised to know that I actually left *Doctor Who* because the BBC and I did not see eye-to-eye over the stories which

The Doctor finds himself at the mercy of the Celestial Toymaker (Michael Gough) and the clowns Clara (Carmen Silvera) and Joey (Campbell Singer)

were being proposed for the future – I thought there was too much evil entering into the spirit of the programme.

Doctor Who had been spelled out to me as a children's programme, and I very much wanted it to stay as such. I particularly wanted to see characters from famous children's books coming into it. But, I am afraid, the BBC had other ideas – and so I left. Which was all the more of a shame because for some time they had been saying they would keep the show going as long as I was willing to play it!

However, it is a long time ago now, and I think my hurt has healed, although I must say the events of those last few months are engraved on my heart. For, you know, I don't think you can ever escape from the character – that's the agony of being Doctor Who!

There was lots of fun being the Doctor, of course, especially with all the children who seemed to love him. For my part I loved all the letters, some of which were addressed to Mr Who and even Uncle Who!

I often had fun with the journalists who interviewed me, and I used to like answering the phone in a muffled voice. At this, the reporter at the other end would invariably say, 'Who?' To which I would reply with a chuckle, 'Yes, that's right – *Doctor* Who!'

It has also been gratifying that a number of people – including my successor in the role as the Doctor – have said some very kind things about my performance, and it is nice to know that the programme goes on, although somewhat differently from the original idea. And because it is now being shown in places like Australia, New Zealand and Canada and its audience is getting bigger every week, I am sure it will go on for many more years.

I do still wonder, though, where we might all have been today if *The Son of Doctor Who* had been made!

(From an interview given by William Hartnell to John Ball in April 1969, following the news that his successor, Patrick Troughton, was leaving the programme, and a third Doctor was about to be named.)

EARLY DAYS IN THE TARDIS

DAVID WHITAKER, the first script editor of Doctor Who, *has been described by the Producer, Verity Lambert, as 'indispensible' in the creation and ultimate success of the series. Much respected by writers and actors alike, David had come to his job on the embryo show after years spent as an actor, director, producer, then BBC script writer (from 1957), and finally as a script editor. Although he lived long enough to see* Doctor Who *become an international success, his death in February 1980 robbed television of a great talent. The following essay is compiled from various interviews David gave to journalists from newspapers and magazines including John Sandilands of the* Daily Mail, *Jack Bell of the* Daily Mirror *and* TV World.

WORKING ON *Doctor Who* was a bit like life in the TARDIS – you could never be quite sure where you were going next! For this reason in the early days I set up a kind of pool of writers, people who were my friends, or friends of friends. This meant I had writers I could trust not only to produce a good story within the restrictions we had to live with, but could also keep to very tight deadlines.

I found that writers had to be divided into those who could write about the past, and those who set their stories in the future. Strangely, very few could do both. There were those who thought the futuristic stories would be easier because the scope was so wide, but in fact we had to set quite strict limits so that everything remained at least reasonably plausible!

Considering what the BBC usually spent on serials in the Sixties, we had a very reasonable budget indeed. Obviously the programme controllers had been convinced by Sydney Newman's enthusiasm, but this put a lot of pressure on the producer, Verity Lambert, and myself. We were both terribly excited about the faith that had been shown, but also terribly nervous in case we failed.

I think that nowadays people find it very hard to imagine just how much commitment is required working on a television series. Especially one like *Doctor Who* which, in its first year, was committed to a run of 52 episodes. And we had the added burden of trying to create illusions with the limited technical resources of the time.

Unlike other shows where the sets and costumes can usually be drawn from props, most of ours had to be made from scratch. Ray Cusick who headed our design team produced some absolute miracles out of cellophane paper and battery bulbs!

I had to be more than just a story editor too. With Verity, I played an active part in the whole production. I would often have to liase with props, advise the designers and then sit down to thrash out storylines with the writers.

I always went to as many rehearsals and recordings as I could, and it soon became evident that William Hartnell was a brilliant choice as the Doctor. There is no doubt in my mind that he secured the success of the series for us. He was exactly right: formidable, and a little remote.

Above and opposite: Two shots from the pilot episode of 'An Unearthly Child', the very first Doctor Who story

People have asked me why the first Doctor was such a remote figure, and I have argued that that was the strength of his character. It gave the audience an immediate respect for everything he did and said – he was a kind of father figure.

I always wanted there to be an aura of mystery around him that underlined the question which is posed by the title of the series. Now, of course, we've learned a lot more about the Doctor, and though I can appreciate that discovering all about a character is an essential part of any long-running series, it still seems to me a shame that a lot of the mystery has gone.

Looking back, it was a tremendous feeling when the show became a success. For a time it dominated all our lives, and there was very much a sense of belonging to a family – a Space Family Who! I remember getting very concerned about the Doctor's life style in the TARDIS and in one story wrote a lengthy sequence about the food machine used by the space-travellers. It was unnecessary, I suppose, and was cut out – but it showed how the series had taken me over!

It also helped when I ran into a problem at the end of the first season. A script had not materialised, and the choice was either to take the series off the air until it was ready or else I had to write a filler using the sets we had in stock.

A TARDIS-bound story with no guest cast

was the obvious solution, but it was a horrendous prospect for me! I remember I spent about two days and nights writing 'The Edge of Destruction'. It was a bit of a nightmare, in more ways than one, and though it seemed to go down well with the audience, it rather confused the cast who knew their characters but couldn't quite grasp the totally discontinuous way in which I had to make them behave!

Of course, no discussion of the early days of *Doctor Who* would be complete without a mention of my good friend Terry Nation and the Daleks. Ironically, he didn't want to write for us to begin with, considering it rather demeaning that he had even been asked! However, in the end the collapse of another job persuaded him to go ahead and do something for us. That turned out to be 'The Daleks' – and with it came two things.

The first was a row. The second – audiences of an incredible number!

The row came about because certain people at the BBC thought that the Daleks were puerile and would drag the show down. And, as one of our prime intentions was to keep an educational slant to the programme, they were not felt to be in the right mould at all.

Actually, of course, 'The Daleks' *was* educational and in a rather subtle way – it showed the dangers of war, pacifism and racial hatred, as well as containing many admirable and idealistic truths. The show was also a jolly good adventure story!

At any rate, we were allowed to go ahead and make the story, simply because there was no other script ready! And when it was shown, not very long after being recorded, we were proved right.

As a matter of interest, we did not intend to bring the Daleks back. I felt very strongly that we should search constantly for new ideas. As it turned out, the huge popularity of the Daleks in fact blackmailed us into commissioning a sequel. The Daleks were a smashing invention, and I took to them at once. I would say they are worthy of Jules Verne!

Not long afterwards I collaborated with Terry on a stage play, *The Curse of the Daleks*, which was produced at the Wyndham Theatre in London during the Christmas period of 1965. Because the BBC held the copyright in *Doctor Who*, the Doctor himself could not appear, nor the companions or even the TARDIS. Instead, Terry and I introduced the members of an Earth spacecraft who have been forced down onto Skaro, the home planet of the Daleks. There the two heroes try and find out why the ship has been drawn to Skaro and who among their fellow crew-members is in league with the Daleks in another of their terrible plots to destroy humanity.

Despite the very severe limitations of the stage, I thought the play succeeded quite well, and I had a little fun writing the 'history' of the Daleks for inclusion in the programme! [The article is also reprinted in this book.]

I was also approached to write a novelisation of Terry's first story, 'The Daleks'. Once I accepted, though, I found I had taken on an incredible amount of work because the whole of Terry's story had to be re-structured and largely re-written to make it work as a novel, as distinct from a television play. I was quite pleased with the result which, of course, has proved the forerunner of other such novelisations.

I also enjoyed writing 'Evil of the Daleks' (1967) because it included a theme I am very fond of – the lure of alchemy. It was a good opportunity to write an atmosphere story and I had some pleasing characters to work with.

Interestingly, too, it was intended to be the final Dalek story, as Terry Nation wanted to launch them in America. Somehow, though, I didn't really think they would be gone for good!

THE DALEK
CHRONICLES

Roberta Tovey who played Susan in the two
Dalek films with friends

As you know, Terry Nation discovered and translated the Dalek Chronicles. The story of how those Chronicles came to light is interesting in itself. This is how it was.

About two years ago, I was at home writing when Terry telephoned me and asked if he could talk over something. I was delighted to hear from him and agreed at once. An hour later, we settled down in chairs with a tray of coffee and sandwiches between us.

Terry took a small cube from his pocket and handed it to me, asking for my opinion of it.

I examined it curiously. It was twice the size of a lump of sugar, entirely made of glass except for a small collection of little compartments at its centre. I shook my head in bewilderment and returned it to him, confessing myself baffled.

'I found it in my garden,' he said, 'and, out of curiosity, I drilled a hole through it to its centre. A number of slivers of metal fell into the palm of my hand. I magnified them and found them to be microfilms!'

It was then that he told me of the planet Skaro, set in the next Universe but one, and of one of the races inhabiting it, the kindly, graceful and peace-loving people called the Thals. I learned of dead forests and a lake of mutations, a brilliant city rising out of a desert.

And I also heard of the other race on that planet – the inhuman, terrifying creatures called Daleks; sworn enemies of all humanity.

If you wonder why it is that all the adventures and stories of the Daleks are set well into the future, you must realise that what Terry discovered are capsules containing histories of the future. What curve of time is responsible for this, neither of us can tell you.

Are the glass cubes sent down by some friendly planet deliberately, as a warning to us? Or has some Dalek History Museum exploded violently in space, showering the stream of time by accident with information that Daleks must want to keep secret?

Perhaps it is enough that we *do* know, and can prepare ourselves.

Since that day, more of the little cubes have come to light and Terry and I have sometimes worked together, so anxious has our world become to know as much about the alien race as it can.

The play, *The Curse of the Daleks*, for example, is the result of our collaboration – a translation we have worked on from a cube discovered in Kensington Gardens. We both believe there are other glass cubes in existence, hidden, perhaps, in a clump of grass or lying at the base of a tree.

When you are out in your garden, or in the park, do remember to keep your eyes open, won't you?

(*Written by David Whitaker in December 1965 to coincide with the opening of the play,* The Curse of the Daleks, *which he wrote in conjunction with Terry Nation for staging at Wyndham's Theatre in London.*)

Dalek in transit at London's King's Cross Station
Opposite: Davros, the Daleks' maniacal creator as played by Michael Wisher

THE DALEK
MASTER PLANS

The dreaded mutations met disaster on Spiridon;
a scene from 'Planet of the Daleks'

'HEY TRUNDLED menacingly out of the imagination of a furniture-salesman turned script writer into the folklore of the twentieth century. Aided by the ingenious imagination of a brilliant designer and the determination of a young producer, they defied the initial opposition of the BBC hierarchy to create delicious fear as well as an enduring fascination amongst three generations of young – and not so young – television viewers. They are the Doctor's greatest enemies – *the Daleks*!'

From *The Secret Book of Davros*.

A COMPLETE DALEK INDEX

1 'The Daleks' by Terry Nation (1963)
Location: The planet Skaro.
Dalek Task Force: Five (Robert Jewell, Kevin Manser, Michael Summerton, Gerald Taylor, Peter Murphy). *Dalek Voices*: Peter Hawkins and David Graham.
Collaborators: The Doctor's granddaughter, Susan (unwittingly).
Special note: This hugely influential story which ensured the success of Doctor Who on television, was later the basis of a feature film, *Doctor Who and the Daleks*, made in 1965, and starring Peter Cushing as the Doctor.

2 'The Dalek Invasion of Earth' by Terry Nation (1964)
Location: Earth.
Dalek Task Force: Five (Robert Jewell, Gerald Taylor, Nick Evans, Kevin Manser, Peter Murphy). *Dalek Voices*: Peter Hawkins and David Graham.
Collaborators: Robomen and Slaves. Also Slyther (Nick Evans) the Dalek's man-eating creature.
Special note: This story was the basis of the second feature length movie, *Daleks – Invasion Earth 2150 AD*, made in 1966 and also starring Peter Cushing as the Doctor.

3 'The Chase' by Terry Nation (1965)
Location: The planet Aridus; the Empire State Building, New York; The *Mary Celeste* ship;

Tom Baker as the fourth Doctor in a publicity still with his most persistent enemies

MARTIN O'GORMAN

Haunted House at the Festival of Ghana; and the planet Mechanus.

Dalek Task Force: Four (Gerald Taylor, Kevin Manser, Robert Jewell, John Scott Martin).
Dalek Voices: Peter Hawkins and David Graham.
Collaborators: Robot Doctor (Edmund Warwick), Aridians.
Special note: Appearance of a new creation by Terry Nation, the Mechonoids, played by 'Dalek refugees' Murphy Grumbar, Jack Pitt, John Scott Martin and Ken Tyllson.

4 'Mission to the Unknown' by Terry Nation (1965)
Location: The planet Kembel.
Dalek Task Force: 4 (Robert Jewell, Kevin Manser, Gerald Taylor, John Scott Martin).
Dalek Voices: Peter Hawkins and David Graham.
Collaborators: None
Special note: This single-episode *Doctor Who* story did not feature the Doctor but was intended as a prelude to the next mammoth Dalek adventure . . .

5 'The Dalek's Masterplan' by Terry Nation (with additional material by Dennis Spooner) (1965)
Location: The planets Kembel, Tigus, Mira and Earth.
Dalek Task Force: Four (Robert Jewell, Kevin Manser, Gerald Taylor, John Scott Martin).
Dalek Voices: Peter Hawkins and David Graham.
Collaborators: Mavic Chen (Kevin Stoney), the Meddling Monk (Peter Butterworth).
Special note: With twelve episodes, this is the longest-ever *Doctor Who* story, and widely regarded by the fans as one of the all-time classics.

6 'Power of the Daleks' by David Whitaker (1966)
Location: The planet Vulcan.
Dalek Task Force: Four (Gerald Taylor, Kevin

The TARDIS crew find themselves prisoners of the Daleks and the Aridians in this scene from 'The Chase'

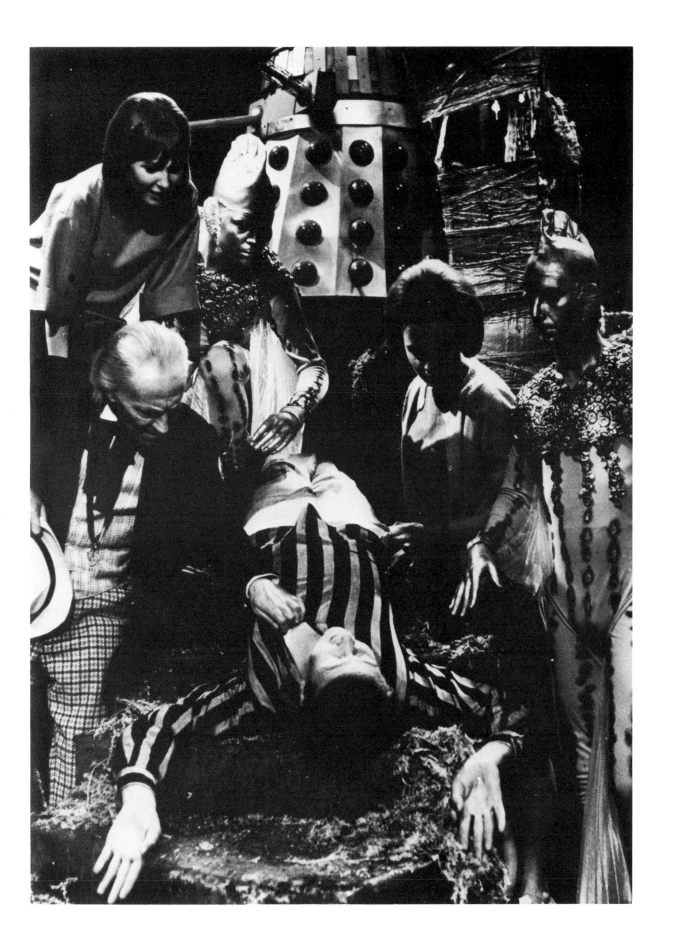

Manser, Robert Jewell, John Scott Martin).
Dalek Voice: Peter Hawkins.
Collaborators: Chief Scientist Lesterson (Robert James).
Special note: This story introduced the new regeneration of the Doctor, Patrick Troughton, in the first Dalek story not to have been written by Terry Nation; David Whitaker had, though, been the Script Editor for Terry's original stories.

7 'Evil of the Daleks' by David Whitaker (1967)
Location: Earth and the planet Skaro.
Dalek Task Force: Four (Robert Jewell, Gerald Taylor, Murphy Grumbar, John Scott Martin).
Dalek Voices: Peter Hawkins and Roy Skelton.
Collaborators: Edward Waterfield (John Bailley).
Special note: Gatwick Airport was used as the real-life location for the theft of the TARDIS at the beginning of this almost contemporary Dalek story!

8 'Day of the Daleks' by Louis Marks (1972)
Location: Earth.
Dalek Task Force: Chief Dalek (John Scott Martin). *Dalek Voices*: Oliver Gilbert and Peter Massaline.
Collaborators: Ogron (Rick Lester).
Special notes: After an absence from the screen of five years, the Daleks return in full colour for the first time and to combat the third Doctor, Jon Pertwee.

9 'Planet of the Daleks' by Terry Nation (1973)
Location: The planet Spiridon.
Dalek Task Force: Four (Tony Starr [Dalek Supreme], John Scott Martin, Murphy Grumbar, Cy Town). *Dalek Voices*: Roy Skelton and Michael Wisher.
Collaborators: None.
Special notes: Like Sir Arthur Conan Doyle returning to writing stories of his creation, Sherlock Holmes, Terry Nation again creates a new Dalek story for the third Doctor, having been unable to launch them in America as stars of their own TV series.

10 'Death to the Daleks' by Terry Nation (1974)
Location: The planet Exxilon.
Dalek Task Force: Three (John Scott Martin, Murphy Grumbar, Cy Town). *Dalek Voices*: Michael Wisher.

Collaborator: Zombie (Steven Ismay).
Special notes: Terry Nation reveals that although he invented the word Dalek, there is an identical word in Serbo-Croat that most appropriately means 'far and distant things'!

11 'Genesis of the Daleks' by Terry Nation (1975)
Location: Planet Skaro.
Dalek Task Force: Five (Michael Wisher [Davros], John Scott Martin, Max Faulkner, Keith Ashley, Cy Town). *Dalek Voices*: Roy Skelton.
Collaborators: Kaleds (Richard Reeves, Peter Mantle).
Special notes: The fourth Doctor, Tom Baker, meets his oldest enemies, in a story Terry Nation considers one of his best – particularly because of the new character he introduces: Davros, the creator of the Daleks.

12 'Destiny of the Daleks' by Terry Nation (1979)
Location: The planet Skaro.
Dalek Task Force: Three (David Gooderson as Davros, Cy Town, Mike Mungarvan).
Dalek Voices: Roy Skelton.
Collaborators: Enslaved humans.
Special notes: This return of the Daleks also coincided with a new companion for the fourth Doctor in the shape of Lalla Ward, destined to become 'Mrs Who' – the wife of Tom Baker.

13 'Resurrection of the Daleks' by Eric Saward (1984)
Location: Earth.
Dalek Task Force: Five (Terry Molloy as Davros, John Scott Martin, Cy Town, Tony Starr, Toby Byrne). *Dalek Voices*: Brian Miller and Royce Mills.
Collaborators: Lytton (Maurice Colborne).
Special notes: The thirteenth encounter between the Doctor and the Daleks does not prove unlucky for the fifth Doctor, Peter Davison, in his last season as the Time Lord – despite newspaper speculation that this two-part story by the show's Script Editor might see the end of one or other of them!

14 'Revelation of the Daleks' by Eric Saward (1985)
Location: The planet Necros.

ALAN ROWLEY

Dalek Task Force: Five (Terry Malloy as Davros, John Scott Martin, Cy Town, Tony Starr, Toby Byrne). *Dalek Voices*: Roy Skelton and Royce Mills.
Collaborators: Jobel (Clive Swift).
Special notes: The sixth and latest Doctor, Colin Baker, has an early introduction to his old foes in another two part story by Eric Saward, which also brings back Davros once again. Although the Doctor finds that life and death become confused for him on the planet Necros, there is no confusing the signs that the Daleks will be making a fifteenth appearance in the future . . .

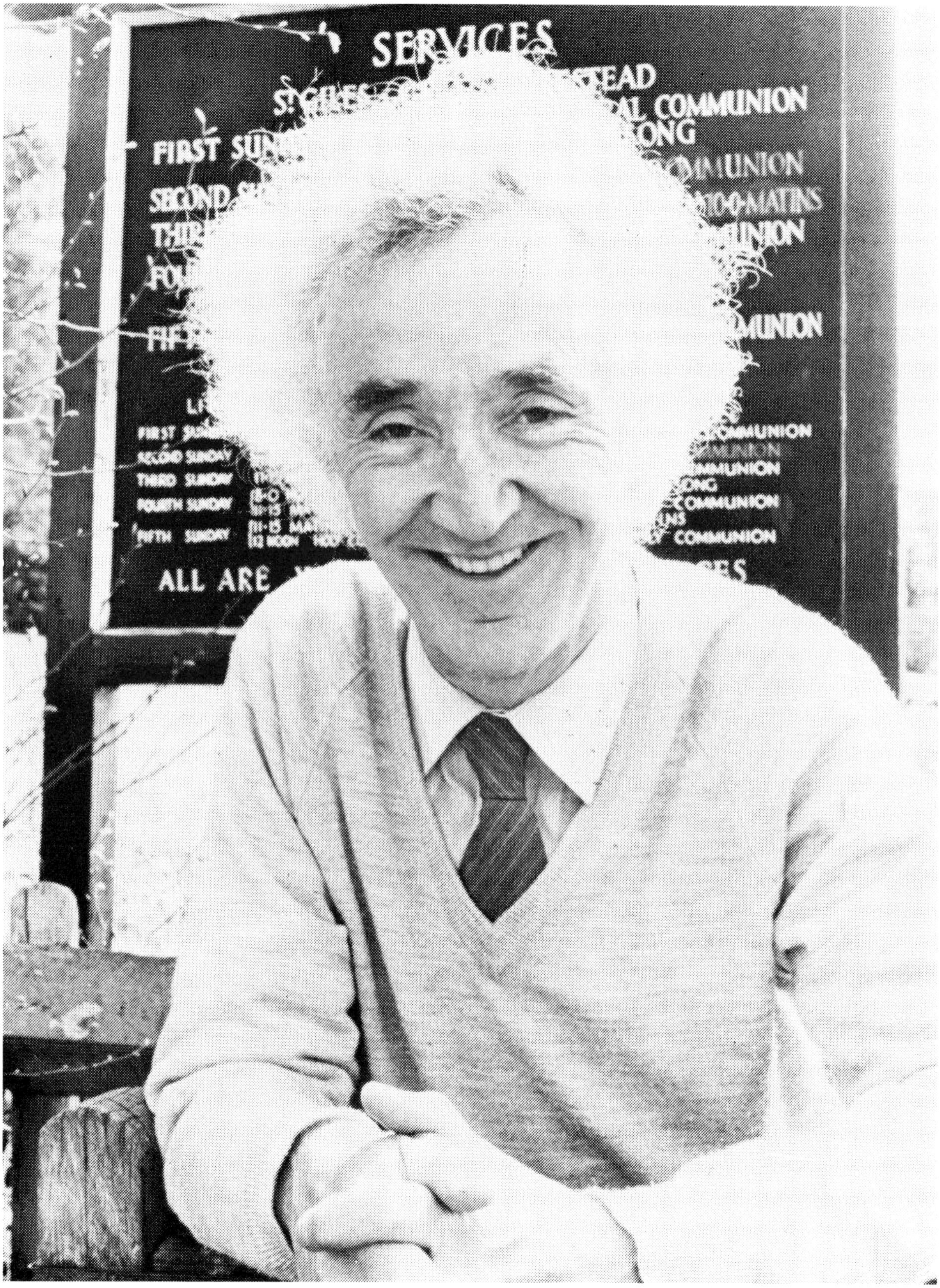
SERVICES
COMMUNION
ALL ARE

THE LIFE OF A DALEK

JOHN SCOTT MARTIN has been described by The Sun as 'the Number One Dalek' and certainly in twenty years of playing the Doctor's most famous and enduring adversary, he has experienced just about every kind of drama both in front of the cameras and behind them! A Liverpudlian by birth, John describes himself as a character actor who can play anything from 'an archbishop to an alcoholic'. In his career he has been a singer, pantomime artist and stage star as well as appearing in numerous other television serials apart from Doctor Who. It is, though, as a Dalek that he has become famous, and he has made numerous public appearances as 'The Supreme Dalek'. In real life, he is a quietly amusing man and a dedicated churchgoer. He has also set up a business with his wife hiring out costumes in the Suffolk area where he lives. Here, though, he talks about what life is really like for himself and the other little group of men who play those 'ruthless monsters without a redeeming feature', as their creator, Terry Nation, once called them . . .

IT WAS Richard Martin, who directed some of
the earliest *Doctor Who* shows including the
second Dalek story, 'The Dalek Invasion of
Earth' in 1964, who was responsible for
trundling me into a life of 'Exterminate!
Exterminate!'

In 1964 I appeared in a *Z Cars* story for the
BBC which he directed. After we had finished,
we got talking and he told me his next project
was a science-fiction show called *Doctor Who*. I
thought nothing more about it, until a few days
later when he rang me and asked if I would go
and have a chat with him.

Little did I know what that chat was going to
lead to!

Richard told me he was looking for people to
cast in his *Doctor Who* story called 'The Web
Planet'.

'I'd like you to play a monster,' he said very
matter-of-factly. 'You won't be seen, but your
name will be credited. It is, though, a rather
strange monster called a Zarbi.'

I suppose I should have been suspicious right
there and then, but he was persuasive and I
agreed.

The Zarbi was described to me as a kind of
huge ant, but when I saw this construction of
fibre glass and steel I knew I was in for
problems. In fact, it was rather like standing in a
single wardrobe with your feet out of the bottom
and your head out of the top! It was a terrible
costume to wear – and on reflection it made a
Dalek seem like a velvet evening dress!

Anyhow, I got on with the job. It was not like
playing Hamlet, of course, and if anything it was
rather like playing a pantomime horse! But I
thought if I played it seriously it would entertain
the kids and as I had never done that before and
always wanted to, it perhaps wasn't such a bad
thing.

How wrong can you be! Playing that Zarbi
was six weeks of hell – toddling around in a
crouching position inside a steel and fibre glass
shell. You couldn't stand upright when you were
in it because its tail was longer than you were. So
the only way to become upright was to get on a
twelve-inch riser block and tuck your 'tail' over
the end. Do you know, to this day whenever I
see one of those blocks in a studio I still call
them 'Zarbi Blocks'!

Anyhow, one night, almost at the end of the

John Scott Martin and the current team of Dalek operators;
Clockwise: Cy Town, Toby Burn, Tony Star
Opposite: The Daleks' Achilles' Heel as seen by Punch

recording, I thought to myself I've got to straighten my back just once. So up I stood, over I tipped, and I finished up like a crab on its back on the sea shore with my legs in the air!

'Stop the recording!' I heard someone shout.

'John, John!' the voice went on more urgently. 'Are you all right?'

Someone seemed to think I might have killed myself.

'Yes,' I replied at last. 'Leave me alone – I'm more comfortable than I've been for weeks!'

Despite this unpromising first association with *Doctor Who*, Richard talked me into appearing in his next show in the series, 'The Chase'. I had two parts, in fact, as one of the robots called Mechonoids, and also for the first time, a Dalek.

That seemingly unimportant casting changed my life. It seems impossible, but it was twenty years ago, and ever since then I have stayed with the programme and appeared with all six Doctors. And, actually, I only became a Dalek because one of the actors who had played the part in the earlier two stories dropped out!

For a while I was the new boy, because the other Daleks, Kevin Manser, Gerry Taylor and Robert Jewell, had done it before and they knew

how things were done. But it didn't take long for me to get the hang of operating the equipment.

Although the programme never went out live, it was almost like a live performance in the early days. I remember we used to rehearse from Monday to Thursday and then record on Friday night, almost as a non-stop performance, taking about an hour and a half. It was also structured so that if the Daleks had to hurtle from one end of the studio to another for a scene, everyone would help them. For us inside, it was a case of picking up our skirts and running!

Being inside a Dalek is more like sitting in a wheel-chair or bubble car. Your rubber-soled feet are out of the bottom and you have to use them to provide the propulsion. Some people think they have motors, but let me assure you they do *not* – nor do they work by magic! Just sheer hard work by the operator's feet!

I am about five foot nine inches tall and I don't think anybody taller could manage a Dalek. It is in two parts, and the top section, just about fits over me when I am seated. In the top you have the controls for the lights which flash in synchronisation with the voice.

In fact, we are not linked in any way to the voices of the Daleks which you hear on screen. All we can do in the Dalek's casing is see and hear what the other people on the set are doing. We are there very much as actors, and it is a question of us learning the lines and playing them by pressing the button to activate the lights.

The 'voice' of the Dalek, who is positioned at the other end of the studio, has to work in speed with my lights, just as I try to work in time with his voice. It is essential we work in as close harmony as possible.

I believe that in the early days there were plans that the actors in the Daleks should do the voices. But I gather it was felt that if another actor had to stand close to a Dalek while speaking, there was a danger the microphone might not be able to separate the voices and the actor would end up sounding like a Dalek! So a team of off-stage actors including Peter Hawkins, Roy Skelton and others were assembled to play the voices.

Of course, for interviews and personal appearances as a Dalek I do the voice myself, but under studio conditions this is just not possible.

Also in the roof is the control of the Dalek's eye-stick. Similarly guns belching out smoke or, more recently, laser beams. Occasionally we have even had good old-fashioned machine guns with bullets firing which can be fearfully noisy for those inside!

There is also the famous 'sink plunger' which everyone laughs at. But that has proved most useful for opening and closing doors – or even touching up make-up girls who are passing by! Sometimes the plungers have been taken off and trays fitted so that the Daleks can carry small pieces of equipment about on them and appear to be giving them to other actors.

Over the years we have even had smoke cannisters inside the Daleks fixed under the seat, so that they could belch out smoke at the appropriate time.

I also remember one glorious occasion when rubber bags of what I can only call 'goo' were fitted on the inside of the Dalek lids just above our heads. In them were chopped-up foam rubber, make-up paste, paint and all sorts of horrible things. The idea was that, when each of us was destroyed, we would push our heads up against the rubber bags and the Dalek's brains and gore would just flow out onto the studio floor.

Now this worked fine when we were not actually *doing* it during rehearsal. But when we came to the real thing in front of the cameras, the studio floor was immediately knee-deep in gore, looking rather like a gâteau gone wrong. Then we found we couldn't move – for the poor little Daleks' feet just kept slipping on the floor!

That was certainly one of our less successful experiments on *Doctor Who*!

One of the amusing things about being a Dalek is that often when you are on the set, people forget that you are inside. Especially during those seemingly interminable periods when you are waiting to shoot a scene.

Even years after the Daleks had become famous, there were still members of the BBC staff who would come onto the set and be absolutely amazed when an actor stepped out from inside one! Sometimes people even stood beside us chatting, and when we suddenly joined in the conversation they would jump six feet in the air!

On occasions I've overheard people being terribly indiscreet about other members of the cast – even the director or producer. I can tell you that being a Dalek can sometimes give you perfect material for blackmail!

"Well, this certainly buggers our plan to conquer the Universe."

There were times when people actually *working* on the show forgot we were in there – and this could be a real problem because it is impossible to get out on your own due to the weight of the top half. Then you have to scream and holler.

I can well remember at the end of several recording sessions when I was suddenly aware that everyone was on the point of going home. Then it was a case of shouting loudly, 'Daleks – Out! For God's sake get us out!'

Mind you, it is nice being a Dalek on location in the winter. For when the other actors have to hang around freezing you can sit comfortably inside your machine, cosy and warm, and read a newspaper or book!

That also reminds me of the time when things almost got *too* hot. For a particular scene, two of us, Kevin Manser and I, had some pyrotechnics like fireworks draped around our Daleks and little batteries inside to trigger them off at the right moment. We were to hurtle down a corridor with smoke belching out.

Both of us thought we would have problems seeing where we were going as well as being choked by the smoke. The props department came up with the answer, though – World War One gas masks. The face-pieces would protect our eyes and the tube could be stuck out of the side of the Dalek in order to breathe.

Theory – fine. Practice – no good at all! Because the smoke that went out of the Dalek came straight back up the tube!

So there we were, Kevin and I, coughing and spluttering, blind as bats, hurtling along this corridor. Well, of course, we crashed into each other and the tops of the Daleks lifted up – just at the very moment when we fired off the explosions! Poor Kevin's shirt caught on fire and I was in similar danger. Fortunately, the firemen who were standing by nipped in smartly and we came to no harm.

But after all this, the director just said briskly, 'OK, lads. Get cleaned up. Then we'll just have to do it again!'

There were always problems when we went out of the studios. We shot some scenes in a

quarry where they mine Fuller's Earth near Reigate. Now, everyone knew the Daleks wouldn't be able to travel very quickly over this kind of terrain, so it was decided to put down railway lines like those used for the cameras, and also little wheels on the bottom of the Daleks. The idea was that we should be really mobile Daleks – the like of which you had never seen before. Or since.

For what happened, of course, was that we belted down the straight and as soon as we came to a bend in the line we fell off!

It was just as difficult on ordinary streets and roads. Even the cracks in the pavements could give us problems. And I also recall trouble trying to get over Westminster Bridge which I had always thought was flat. Believe you me, it

KILL THE DOC-TOR

Things hot up for a Dalek when attacked by Exxilons in 'Death to the Daleks'

A. CHILD

EDINBURGH FESTIVAL Fringe '84

Middleham Theatre Company

LATEST PLAY BY RICHARD FRANKLIN

NEWS FLASH!

DR. WHO GRAPPLES WITH MRS. THATCHER ON THE FALKLANDS!

the original T.V. Cast

in

"RECALL U.N.I.T."

or

"THE GREAT TEA BAG MYSTERY"

BBC T.V. Dr. Who/Richard Franklin © 1984

with guest appearance on August 24th

THE SUPREME DALEK! — John Scott Martin

at the Playhouse Theatre, Edinburgh

Venue 59, 18-22 Greenside Place, Edinburgh

August 20th - 25th   10.30 a.m. & 2.30 p.m.

(Reduced Price Public Previews - August 17th & 18th at 2.30p.m.)

BOOK NOW

031-557 2590 (Theatre Box Office)
031-226 5257 (Fringe Box Office)

Welbury Press, Richmond, North Yorkshire

has quite a slope – or at least it does to a Dalek!

There's a lovely cartoon which seems to me to summarise the whole predicament of the Dalek – and it's reprinted here. In my experience even rough ground could halt the Daleks, let alone a flight of stairs!

I have also played a number of other monsters over the years for *Doctor Who*, though perhaps not as many as I might because I think the BBC thought I was getting a fair crack of the whip as a regular Dalek. I do, though, recall being a huge jellyfish, the Nucleus of the Virus, in 'The Invisible Enemy' (1977) in which K9 appeared for the first time, and I was even a human being in one story playing a Welsh miner who died of a terrible disease, caused by the maggots of the Green Death. At rehearsals they called me 'Jones the Maggot'!

I have enjoyed all my time in *Doctor Who*, in fact, because it has brought me in contact with so many interesting people. And also because I have been on a drama contract and treated like any other performer. Even Daleks collect repeat fees, you know!

Although I suppose it has never been easy for any of the Doctors to act with the Daleks – sometimes it must seem a bit like acting with a refrigerator – I have got on well with them all. Don't ask which was my favourite though, for I have always refused to answer that question.

Once, when it was suddenly sprung on me towards the end of a live radio interview, I found the perfect answer. Putting on my best Dalek voice I replied: 'Doctor! Doctor! There is no favourite Doctor! The only favourite Doctor is a *dead* Doctor!'

I think, on reflection, that the secret of the Dalek is that it has been kept such a simple device, and when it is photographed well it is terrifying. It also has the advantage over all the other monsters in that you cannot see the man inside – whereas with everything else from the Cybermen to the Zarbi you just know there is a fellow in there huffing and puffing and sweating his heart out.

And I should surely know after twenty exhausting but never uneventful years!

Opposite: The poster for the famous UNIT play by Richard Franklin (Captain Mike Yates) and featuring John Scott Martin;
Below: Jon Pertwee faces his hated enemies in 'Day of the Daleks'

THE CREATOR
OF THE DALEKS

TERRY NATION is, of course, famous as the man who created the Daleks and gave the series its enduringly popular villains. As is equally well-known, Terry was neither particularly keen to write for the new series when he was first approached, nor did he believe it would last for long. Ironically, too, he had earlier turned down the chance to write scripts for The Army Game *which featured William Hartnell! Nonetheless, he did accept the commission for* Doctor Who – *and his life was never the same again. In the following interview he reveals that it is not the Daleks he considers his best creation – but Davros, in turn the creator of the Daleks!*

MY FAVOURITE character in *Doctor Who* is not, as you might expect in the light of the impact they have had on my life, the Daleks – but Davros, the man in the wheel-chair who has actually perpetuated himself in those machines. He is the creator, you see, and fulfills that old saying: 'You are made in your creator's image.'

I think the set of episodes in which Davros was introduced, 'Genesis of the Daleks' (1975), is outstanding. David Maloney, who was the director, achieved production values for the show that the series hadn't had for ages, and the acting of everyone, especially Michael Wisher as Davros, was excellent.

The battlefield on Skaro where the Doctor and his companions arrived was an astonishing piece of design, too. It was a bizarre, World War One kind of battlefield – because right alongside the most incredible space age gun the viewer saw an iron hatchet!

My inspiration for the story came from something I saw as a kid – a movie based on H. G. Wells's novel *Things To Come*, which was made in 1936 with Raymond Massey and Ralph Richardson. There everybody had reverted almost to primitivism. Technology had run out and they were going back to more and more basic things. But still they were building this great spaceship.

Somewhere, too, there was this corps of elite people who still had their priorities. In fact, I believe that it has already been arranged in our own society that if someone should press the destruction button or release a terrible virus, then there are groups of elitists who will be protected until the very last moment because the future of mankind is in the hands of these elements.

And that's why in 'Genesis of the Daleks' I called Davros's force 'The Elite'.

Survival has, in fact, been a theme that has gone through a lot of my work. I see minefields all around me. I'm a bit like Walter Mitty, really – when I'm in an aeroplane I'm just waiting for the moment when someone says, 'Can anybody fly this plane?'

Now, I know that I *can't*, but I also know that, finally, *I* am going to be the one who has to do it!

I believe there is menace all around us. It's a fairly dark world out there. It doesn't infringe much on my personal life, to be sure – but when

I listen to any news broadcast about, say, Beirut, I think, 'God, I might be living there. I could be one of those people being shelled every day of my life.'

However, as a war-time child, I did grow up when bombs were dropping and men were actually trying to kill me – not me personally, of course, but they wouldn't have minded if they did. I was an only child, too, and spent a lot of time on my own, which is another reason I suppose why I write about lone figures a lot.

When I'm asked about the origins of the Daleks I can similarly trace them back to the wartime period of my life. Although I can't isolate a single character, you could say they sprang collectively from the Nazis. Let me explain.

I have a dream that recurs about once or twice a year. I am driving a car very quickly and the

windscreen is a bit murky. Then, suddenly, the sun shines onto it, and it becomes totally opaque. I'm still hurtling forward at an incredible speed and there's nothing I can see or do, and I can't stop the car.

That's it. Nothing more. Psychologists say the dream can be explained very easily – it's just someone heading for their future. But you don't know what that future is. And however much you plead with somebody to save you from this situation, everybody you go to turns out to be one of *them*. And there's nobody left – you are the loner.

The Daleks are all of 'them' and though they represent different things to different people, everyone sees them basically as government, as officialdom, as that unhearing, unthinking, blanked-out face of authority that will destroy you because it *wants* to destroy you.

The Daleks' schemes approach their horrifying conclusion in this scene from the film 'Daleks: Invasion Earth 2150 AD'

For this reason I have always tried through my writing to make what lies at the end of the road – on the other side of my 'windscreen' if you like – less frightening by making it less unknown and more controllable.

The Doctor always comes out of his crises alive, however bad the problem. The good guys, if they don't win exclusively, at least come out winning their particular round of the war. The Doctor also doesn't win the war – but he does win the battle!

And those are the reasons why, if I am asked from my point of view which was the best *Doctor Who* series ever screened, then Davros and his Elite are my answer.

THE MAN IN THE BATH CHAIR!

MICHAEL WISHER is one of a small group of actors who have appeared in a variety of roles in Doctor Who – *the majority of them heavily disguised as a monster or alien! A former student at RADA he has appeared on the stage in Britain, America and New Zealand in parts ranging from Shakespeare to music hall and pantomime. He has demonstrated similar versatility when appearing on television, where his credits have included* No Hiding Place, Z-Cars *and* Colditz. *Never expecting to become a 'name' in* Doctor Who, *Michael took lightly a prediction made by his friend Tom Baker that, 'Some day you'll become famous for a role that you initially see of little consequence.' These words came dramatically true when fate handed him the role of Davros, the creator of the Daleks, as he here explains . . .*

IF ANYONE imagines it is hard playing Davros in *Doctor Who*, then let me assure them it was twice as hard rehearsing for the part in the first place!

Right from the start I sensed there would be special problems with this half man and half machine. So at the first rehearsal I sat in an antiquated bath chair with a paper bag over my head and two tiny slits for my eyes.

I actually arrived early at the studios to try out the idea before the rest of the cast came in – and when they did arrive they were somewhat amazed to see this paper bag wandering around the place with a strange voice coming out of it!

It was important to rehearse like that, though, because the other actors wouldn't see my face in the real thing, so there would be no expression for them to react to. Only the voice and a blue light to indicate annoyance.

As a matter of fact I wasn't the first choice to play Davros, but apparently someone had the idea that it would be a good thing to hear in Davros the beginnings of a Dalek voice. And as I had performed Dalek voices before, this landed me the job.

When 'Genesis of the Daleks' was being prepared, it was the designer who came up with the idea of Davros looking like a man sitting in half a Dalek. He was supposed to be a very clever scientist who had kept himself alive for 190 years by replacing each part of himself as it died with a bit of machinery!

So his lower half was dead, his left side was dead, and his eyes were dead. In the middle of his forehead was a blue 'eye' which did his seeing, while his hearing was assisted by sensors around his head, and his voice was strained through a microphone.

It was through this that you could hear the beginnings of the Dalek voice. And Davros was simply going through the process to make himself invincible like his creations.

As I have indicated, right from the start I found that there were special problems in playing Davros. It was easy to become disorientated seated in the trolley with the mask on. You can't see properly, you can't hear properly, and though you may think you know your lines perfectly, when it comes to doing them in costume you can dry up because you can't see who you're talking to! It is also very uncomfortable half-crouching inside the trolley, and when I found that wearing trousers made it worse because they rubbed, I opted to wear a kilt!

And if those aren't enough problems, there is also the little matter of going to the loo from time to time. I tried using the blue light to indicate what I wanted. Then in desperation I sneaked a bottle into the costume – but gave the game away when I tipped it over and left little puddles all over the floor!

I looked a pretty bizarre picture during lunch breaks, too. A figure in kilt and gymshoes unable to eat anything through the mask, only take drinks, and I had to use a long cigarette holder if I wanted a smoke to avoid setting fire to myself. I got some *most* peculiar looks!

The masks that are used for *Doctor Who* are made out of a special rubber material and actually have very little breathing space inside. They give you a weird feeling which is quite unnerving, and they also stink! When you wear one for a while, the skin underneath goes white, almost as if you are dead.

This reminds me of an amusing incident filming with Jon Pertwee in 'Terror of the Autons' which was one of my favourites. I had been kept hanging about for the best part of a day in a mask when it finally came to my turn to go before the cameras. I had to rush across a field, be shot by my pursuers and fall down dead.

Now you've got to keep absolutely still for these scenes as the camera closes in. You can't twitch, you must stop breathing and keep your chest from heaving.

Jon then leant down and pulled the mask off. I had to remain absolutely still with my eyes open, but looking upwards. The scene seemed to last for ages and I was beginning to wonder what my face looked like.

I could also see that there was a cloud of doubt creeping into the other actors' eyes. Finally, a voice said waveringly, 'Cut.'

At which one of the cast said apprehensively, 'Is he . . . ?'

Apparently my skin had gone deathly white after all that time under the mask and they thought I actually *was* dead!

I have enjoyed my time in *Doctor Who* and have been lucky enough to play a large variety of roles. I love playing villains particularly – I think I've been dessicated, shot, blown up, eaten, turned into a green mess and mummified. How many *more* ways can there be of dying?

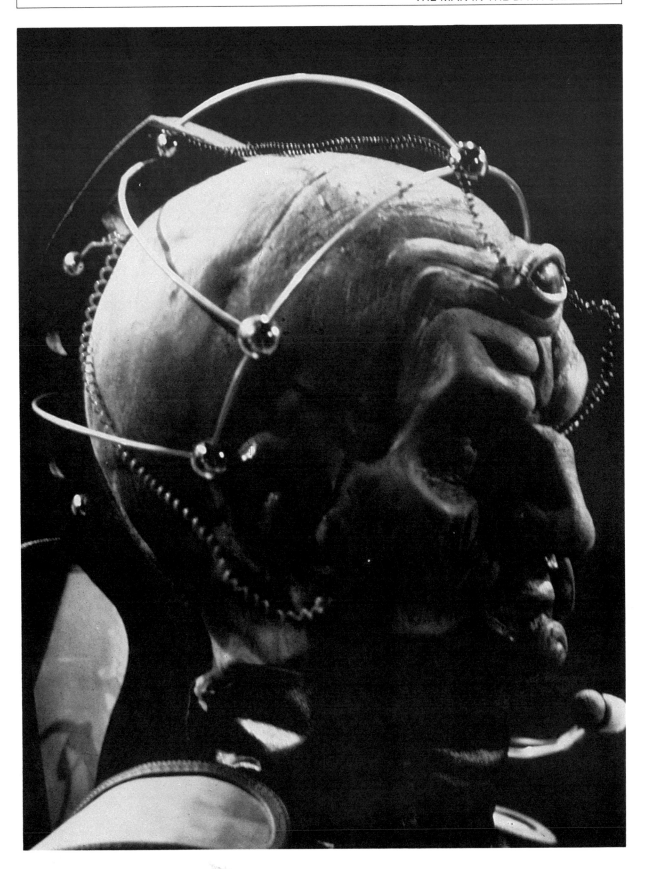

THE SECRET OF WRITING FOR 'DOCTOR WHO'

DENNIS SPOONER *has been described as one of the finest script writers in television. Certainly, in a career spanning over thirty-five years he has written for many of the most famous serials and programmes including* The Avengers, The Professionals, Coronation Street, *and, of course,* Doctor Who, *for whom he served as story editor from 1964 to 1965. As a man who was a stand-up comic in working men's clubs before becoming Harry Worth's joke writer and then breaking into television and film scripting, it is perhaps not surprising that he should have been the man who first introduced an element of humour into* Doctor Who. *He it was also who wrote the final draft of David Whitaker's script for 'Power of the Daleks' (1966) which, of course, introduced Patrick Troughton as the second and more whimsical Doctor. Here he talks about some of the secrets of his craft, with particular relevance to* Doctor Who.

IT HAS BEEN said that my script for 'The Reign of Terror' (1964) was the first *Doctor Who* story to make deliberate use of humour, and certainly it was my intention to introduce a little light-heartedness into the plot.

At that period of its history, each *Doctor Who* story was three hours long – six half-hour episodes – and this inevitably presented the script-writer with problems in episode two. For at this point you don't want to get too much further into the story with things that should happen in episode four.

So humour is the answer. If you can introduce an element of humour through a specific character then it becomes a marvellous way of padding the programme without actually boring the audience or breaking up the plot! The audience will, after all, always watch a 'funny bit' and usually quite like it.

So, in 'The Reign of Terror' I introduced a comic gaoler (played by Jack Cunningham) to break up the action. If he had been a straight gaoler and I had had to involve him for three minutes or so, the result would have been terribly boring.

I believe that humour will always carry a show along, and actors actually like doing humour. It shows them in a different light and proves that they can vary their performances.

Take, for example, a programme about a private detective. Now if he hasn't got various elements in his character and you're making a dozen or so stories, it becomes very much the same after a while. Therefore it is always very satisfying if you can introduce other elements – and if one of these is humour, so much the better.

You do have to be careful, though. Take Raymond Chandler's Philip Marlowe where humour was put in initially to vary the story, and at the end had taken over!

'The Romans' which I wrote for the second season of the series was more of a deliberate attempt to see how far we could go in doing a comedy *Doctor Who*. It was almost *A Funny Thing Happened to the Doctor on the Way to the Forum* story!

What had happened by then was that we had realised the show was now destined to run for a long time. And in television you have to learn very quickly what you are going to get away with, because once a series becomes at all established then you cannot change it.

With the second series of *Doctor Who* we knew that whatever we could establish would mark the boundaries for a long time to come. 'The Romans', as I said, was done for comedy – while in 'The Web Planet', which followed it, we wanted to see how far we could go being weird. And did that show test facilities and technical resources to the limit!

The story went well over budget, but the production was superb. The costumes were a designer's joy. However, though the story got excellent viewing figures – the first episode was actually the highest-placed of the entire season – we decided we would never do anything quite like that again. Not because of the story content, but because of the sheer cost and technical problems involved, plus the fact that in the end we had something that wasn't as sensational as, say, 'The Dalek Invasion of Earth' which looked far more realistic because it featured recognisable landmarks such as the Daleks going over London Bridge. That story certainly set a precedent that has been more or less followed ever since in Dalek stories.

During my period as script editor of *Doctor Who* I always had to keep a close watch on production costs by making sure of getting maximum use of the sets which were built, as well as coping with the problems of actors taking holidays during the series – a thing which they were perfectly entitled to do then with all-the-year-round production. Let me give you an example.

During the making of 'The Crusades' (1965), William Russell wanted to take a week or two's holiday. Now much earlier in the season you have to decide your allocation of so many days for rehearsal, so many days in the studio, and so many days on location. At that time, you see, all the filming for a story was done in a single sequence – even if, in studio time, we were a serial or two ahead.

For 'The Crusades' we need not have had any filming, but because William Russell was going on holiday and because we wanted to have him in all the episodes, the story had to be restructured so that we would see him in the desert for two of the episodes.

Those desert sequences were then filmed as part of the location filming allowance. Which, in turn, meant that certain other scenes which need not have been filmed for technical reasons, were done on film. There was a drawback in that this did limit the amount of film you had available for other serials which might more obviously benefit from its facilities.

As to the actual writing of stories in those early days, if we had a brief it was simply that the Doctor was to be an *observer* of events. If he happened to go into history – or into the future, for that matter – he must never actively interfere with the events in order to change them.

All the William Hartnell programmes were geared towards getting a good story, and the Doctor would arrive and then work within it. I think I would have had a problem with the later stories which always tended to start with the Doctor arriving when there was nothing going on and then making things happen. In other words, he *initiated* the events.

During the early years, most of the stories developed through the Doctor getting into a situation and then trying for the rest of the time to get out of it. For example, he would land the TARDIS because he was in need of something. Then he and the companions would leave the machine, get split up, and on their return find that someone was missing.

'We can't leave,' one or another of the characters would announce, 'until we've found the missing party.'

Thus the whole story, as far as the Doctor was concerned, hinged around trying to rescue whoever was caught, and the subsequent events would centre around their endeavours so to do.

That was certainly what happened in the William Hartnell and Patrick Troughton stories. Tom Baker, on the other hand, would land on a planet, get involved in an adventure, and there would be hundreds of occasions where he could just say, 'I've had enough of this.' And get back into the TARDIS and go!

Before Tom Baker there was always something that kept the Doctor and his friends wherever they might be – other than what was going on around them. It was a fundamental change to decide to have the Doctor influencing the course of events going on around him.

I believe as a result the series has lost some of its original 'realism' when the Doctor was just a time-traveller going around having a look at things. I don't think that if we had only done science-fiction in the early years that *Doctor Who* would have become the success it has.

Someone once said to me at the start of my career, that writing for television is very much like the letter 'W'. A scene works in a 'W', and a programme works in a 'W'. You have to start at the top of the show with something good to 'hook' your audience's interest. Then you can afford to let the plot trickle down to the bottom of the 'W' because the viewers are quite happy to take in some information about the background to the story.

Then, once you've reached the bottom for the first time, you have to write in another 'peak', and having done so allow your viewers time to digest this information before going up to the final climax.

It's a theory that has worked throughout all literature. Take Shakespeare's *Hamlet* which is written almost exactly as television. It starts with the drama of the ghost and Hamlet's father telling our hero that he was murdered. There's the revenge motive all packed into three pages – the all-essential 'hook'. After that there are various peaks building up to the dramatic fight at the end.

That's also the secret of how to write for a series like *Doctor Who* as well!

IS THERE A DOCTOR IN THE HORSE?

DONALD COTTON was the author of the now-legendary Doctor Who *story set in the Wild West called 'The Gun Fighters' (1966) which has been mercilessly attacked by both critics and fans of the programme – none of which has disturbed his good humour. Donald first studied to be a zoologist (an interest he retains to this day), but turned to the Arts after the Second World War and later became both an actor and writer – producing several successful musical reviews and dramas. From 1955 he contributed numerous plays and adaptations to both BBC radio and television, and in 1965 was invited to write for* Doctor Who *by the then-script editor, Donald Tosh. Why this association, which should have paid dividends because of his special knowledge of history, in fact proved rather less than a triumph, he explains here with wry good humour. (As a matter of interest, Donald also helped Verity Lambert devise the series,* Adam Adamant Lives, *and wrote a musical,* My Dear Gilbert *in 1969 about the partnership of Gilbert and Sullivan in which Jon Pertwee played Gilbert!)*

I HAD BEEN asked to play the lead in a try-out production of a one-act play at the Irving Theatre, Leicester Square – closed these many years. And either from disinclination or because I was busy on other matters, I rejected the offer.

Instead, I suggested one Donald Tosh to the management as a replacement – he being then an aspiring actor. He was auditioned, accepted, and played the role with some success. After which, I lost track of him for several years.

Eventually, I learned that he had given up acting and was working as a script editor for the BBC. One day, I was sitting in my local enlarging upon the theme of man's ingratitude to man: people one has tried to help who then forget the circumstances, etc. I am sure you will recognise the Guiness-induced mood I was in! – and I used the above anecdote as an illustration of my thesis.

I returned home, still muttering, and found

waiting for me a telegram from, of all people, Donald – asking If I would be prepared to write for *Doctor Who*!

So, even though such an undertaking was foreign to my previous professional experience, I was so struck by this immediate rebuttal to my argument by the Great Plot-Writer in the Sky,

The Doctor heads for a showdown at the OK Corral in Donald Cotton's 'The Gun Fighters' which achieved the lowest audience figures ever

that I accepted – on condition that I could choose the subject, and bring with me some of the team with whom I had been working on BBC Radio's Third Programme.

The result was 'The Myth Makers' (1965), a story of the Trojan Horse, starring Max Adrian as Priam and with music by Humphrey Searle.

The title of one of the episodes was greeted with bared gums at one script conference – I think it may have been, 'Is There A Doctor In The Horse?' – so a bright apprentice suggested 'Death of a Spy' as a more suitable alternative. At this I pointed out that the plot contained no spy, and therefore his death would be difficult to arrange. They urged me to include one, and have him killed – why not use Tutte Lemkow, who was anyway under contract?

'No time,' I said. 'Dialogue all written and plot constructed to fill twenty-five minutes.'

'Then let's make him a deaf mute, so that he won't take up any time and won't need lines,' they argued.

I reeled in disbelief while they did exactly that – and if you saw the episode, you may have wondered why my friend Tutte flitted pointlessly about the action, looking sinister and confused, under the strange billing of 'Cyclops'. *That* is entirely why!

I wrote 'The Gun Fighters' (1966) next, but by then Donald Tosh – with whom I could work well – was loosening his ties with the series, and I was not allowed so much latitude by the new team. The research for 'The Gun Fighters' was actually done *in* Tombstone, by my old friend and cabaret partner, Tony Snell, who was performing some of our material over there at the time of my writing the piece.

I then devised a new adventure, called 'The Herdsmen of Venus' – the Loch Ness monster being the 'cattle' of Venusian 'farmers' in flying saucers – but this was never transmitted. And probably quite right too!

Word eventually reached my amused colleagues at Broadcasting House that I had done something never to be forgiven. (I can think of no modest way of putting this.) I had considerably raised the 'appreciation figure' of the programme without, however, raising the 'viewing figure', and this could not be tolerated . . .

And so my brief association with *Doctor Who* came to its end!

THE CREATION
OF THE CYBERMEN

GERRY DAVIS, who became Script Editor of Doctor Who *in 1966 towards the end of the Hartnell era, was responsible with the Producer, Innes Lloyd, for moving the series away from the early period costume stories towards the enthralling monster and science-fiction adventures which have remained a staple to the present day. He also played a crucial role in the creation of the Doctor's other favourite foes after the Daleks – the Cybermen. Tracked down to his home in Venice, California, where he continues to write the kind of dramatic and thought-provoking scripts for American television that he once created in England, Gerry here reveals the inside story of how he became known as 'Cyberdad' . . .*

THE CREATION of the Cyberman was the result of what was, looking back, a fairly unique combination of talents and experience.

I had written for theatre, radio, television and films all my life but had little in the way of a scientific education; Doctor Kit Pedler was, successively, a physician, surgeon, pathologist and micro-biologist. He was Head of a Research Department at London University with little connection with the media; his writing had been mainly confined to the twenty-eight brilliant treatises on the retina of the eye that had established his considerable medical and scientific reputation.

We met in the *Doctor Who* offices overlooking Shepherds Bush Green. In the distance the (relatively new then) Post Office Tower dominated the London skyline. Innes Lloyd (the producer) and I (Story Editor) had recently taken over the *Doctor Who* programme and, after a spate of historical programmes (initiated by our predecessors) that sent viewing figures perilously low, had decided that the Doctor had better stick to the future for his adventures – or he wouldn't have one!

Also, one of the staple elements of the programme, the Daleks, had been taken from us by their creator, with a series of feature films in prospect.

So we needed new adversaries for the Doctor and new futuristic adventures – not so easy a task as you might think – the programme had been in operation for three action-packed years and many of the great sci-fi themes had already been explored.

The time had come to break new ground – so I set up meetings with some of the leading popular scientists from Professor Laithwaite of Imperial College, to Alex Comfort (before the sex manuals), to Patrick Moore, the television astronomer, and others of that calibre.

All were, of course, fascinating men to meet, rich in anecdotes, enthralling in conversation but not one of them really rose to the challenge of the *Doctor Who* programme. I used to slyly test them out with questions like: 'An unknown planet emerges to join the solar system and comes into orbit alongside the Earth – it starts to drain the Earth's energy supply – then astronomers notice that it is a reverse image of the Earth . . . what happens next?'

The answers were interesting but usually

A Cybermat, one of the Cybermen's deadly 'pets' who first made their appearance in 'Tomb of the Cybermen'

closed the door to further speculation . . . 'It couldn't happen because!'

Kit Pedler was the last scientist on the list. He had done some work on the last *Quatermass* film – designing the blob-like monster that ended up in Westminster Abbey.

We looked out at the Post Office Tower and I loosed off another favourite idea-starter. 'What if some alien intelligence gets inside the top of the Post Office Tower and decides to take over London; what kind of entity would it be?'

'It would probably be a rogue computer,' said Kit. 'If we use computers to do all our thinking, calculating, designing – even entertaining, exercising, feeding and healing – making all our decisions . . . one day the machines will decide we are a redundant species, like the dinosaurs, and replace us.'

And so it went. I'd met my match: I'd suggest a story proposition and Kit, instead of putting it down, would come up with a way to make it work scientifically. That initial session yielded the idea which later became 'The War Machines' (scripted by Ian Stuart Black).

Meanwhile, with the Daleks removed from

CHRIS SENIOR

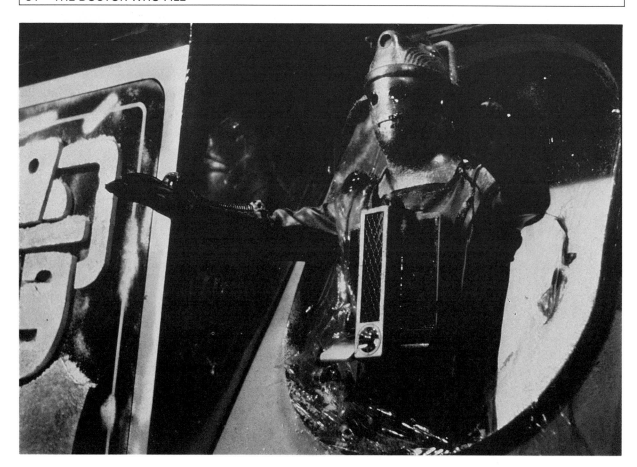

the schedules, we needed a new monster. I asked Kit what his greatest phobia was as a doctor. 'Dehumanising medicine,' he answered. 'You start by providing patients with artificial arms and legs – very necessary and beneficial but what if medical science eventually makes it possible to replace all the human organs – heart, lungs, stomach – with metal and plastic replacements? At which stage would they stop feeling human emotions and become robotic?'

'That's it,' I said. 'Men with everything replaced by cybernetics, lacking the human feelings of love, pity, mercy, fear, compassion and invulnerable to cold or heat. What terrible adversaries they would make! They would be . . .' I think we both said 'Cybermen' together.

'They would be like computers, motivated by pure logic,' said Kit, tapping his apprehension about computers again. 'If it was logical to kill you they would. If you got in their way, however, and did not present a menace to them they would ignore you.'

'But,' I said, 'to be dramatically useful to us

Above: A Cyberman emerges from its frozen tomb on Telos in 'Tomb of the Cybermen'; *Opposite:* two Cybermen confer in the story 'Earthshock' which featured the fifth Doctor

they have to feel some overwhelming driving force. They must be after power: the one ambition left them after they have given up love, sex, appetite, music and beauty.' We contemplated this prospect for a while – both of us enjoyed the good things of life – and shuddered.

'What do they look like?' I asked.

'Ideally,' said Kit, 'they have bodies that change the basic skeleton – for example their arms start from lower down than their elbows – very frightening.'

We started sketching on the blackboard I always install in any office or workroom (to put up ideas and concepts as they occur and, vital to the writer or Story Editor, get them out of your head and visible to yourself and others) and finally had to give up on the dismembered skeleton idea as unworkable. However, by the end of the session, a rough facsimile of what

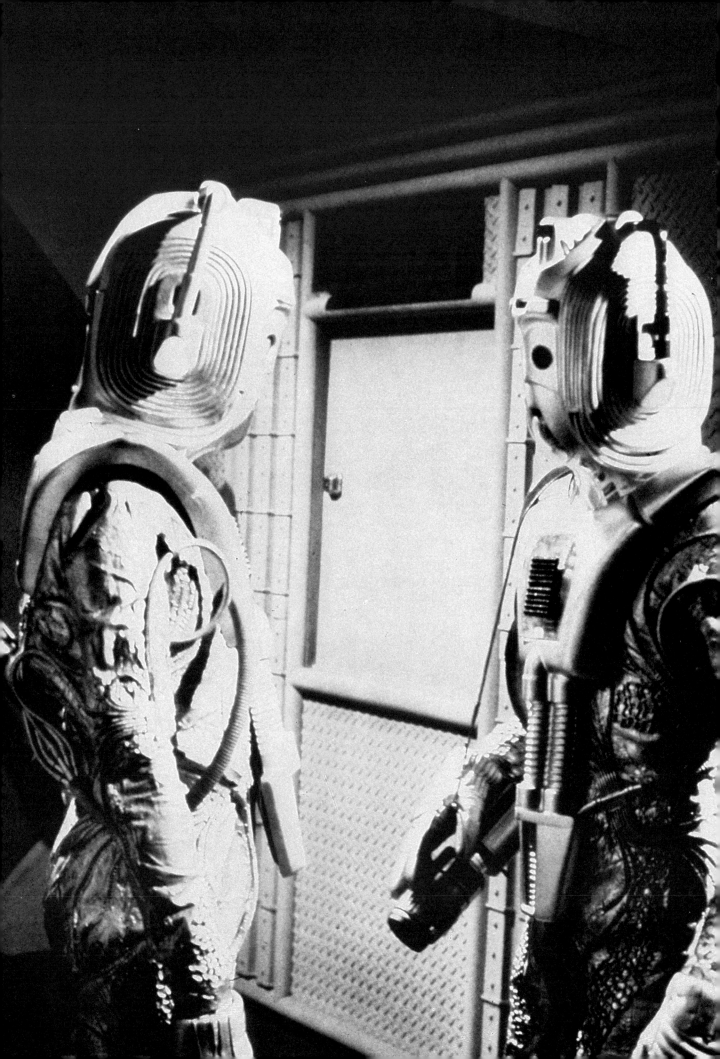

later became the Cybermen had appeared with life-support chest, unit, helmet, boots and a 'cyber-rattle gun' that killed with intense laser beams.

A costume was made in the marvellous BBC Costume Department and the first test of its effect on an unsuspecting public was made. We had someone parade in a Cyberman suit through a busy South London street market. The result was not exactly Earth-shattering. No one ran away in panic – though one natty, middle-aged city gent in bowler and pinstripes stuck his tongue out at the silver giant. Best comment was by a fruit and veg seller who said, 'Must be an advert for one of them kitchen cleaners, Ethel!'

Luckily, nobody associated them with kitchen cleaners when they made their first appearance on *Doctor Who*, looming menacingly out of a blizzard at an American South Polar Base in 'The Tenth Planet' serial (which was jointly written by Kit and myself but credited solely to Kit for internal, BBC policy reasons).

The public reaction to 'The Tenth Planet' was really terrific. Viewing figures soared from three to ten million. The future of *Doctor Who*, which had looked very shakey, was assured and there was an immediate demand for more Cybermen stories.

Further Cyberman adventures – 'The Moonbase' and 'The Tomb of the Cybermen' – quickly followed and Kit and I formed a writing partnership that led to the very successful *Doomwatch* TV series, a feature film and three novels (published in nine languages).

We never lost our affection for our first creation, the Cyberman, though we were unable to write many more Cyberman series owing to other commitments. The Cybermen suits changed from costume designer to costume designer but they always retained their initial menace. (N.B. The first Cybermen adventures were actually banned in Australia for being too gruesome for Aussie TV.)

Kit Pedler, my friend and colleague, very sadly, died prematurely in 1982 and I am the sole surviving 'Cyberdad' as the US *Doctor Who* fans like to call me.

VITALY SABSAY

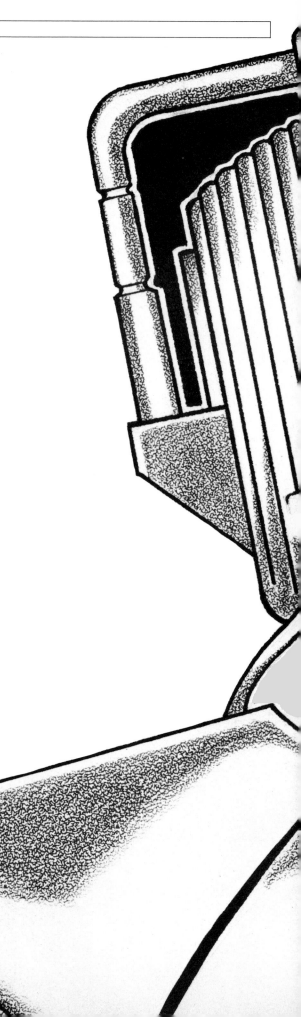

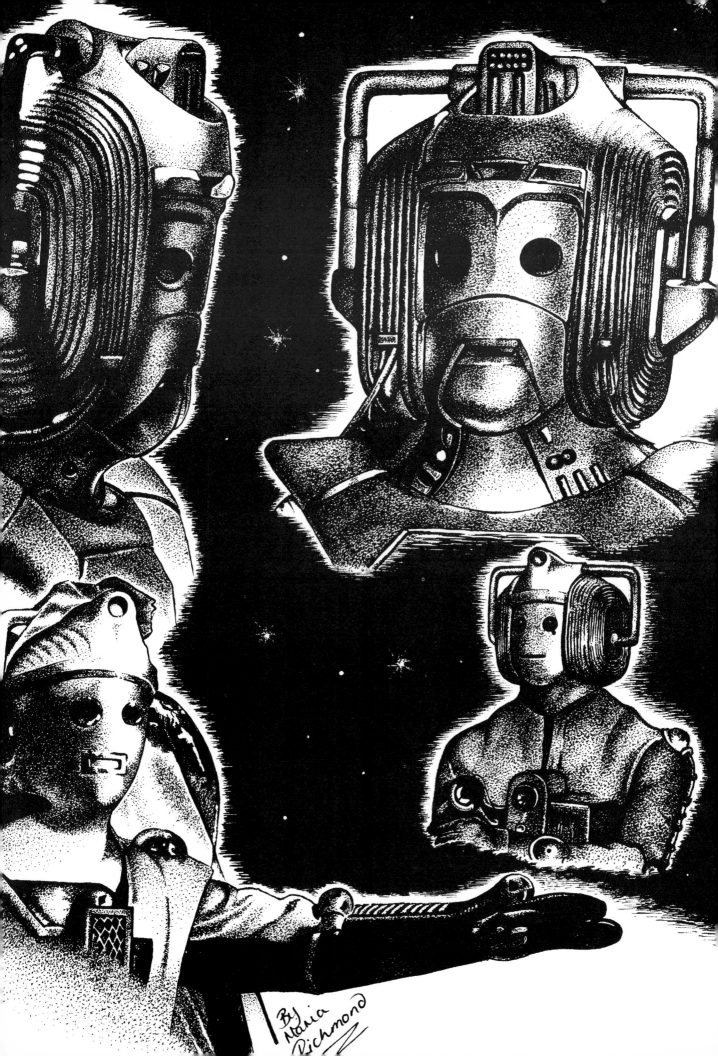

By
Maria
Richmond

MARIA RICHMOND

1 'The Tenth Planet' by Kit Pedler and Gerry Davis (1966)
Location: South Pole Tracking Station.
Contingent: Six original Cybermen – indicated by noses on the faces and two thousand watt lightbulb on top of their heads. Also they are dependent on power from their original planet, Mondas, the twin of Earth. (Actors: Harry Brooks, Reg Whitehead, Greg Palmer. Voices: Peter Hawkins and Roy Skelton.)
Operation and Outcome: To take control of the Earth and use a Z-bomb to destroy the planet. Also to take captive human beings to Mondas for transition into Cybermen. In depriving them of the power from Mondas to stay alive, the Doctor himself is also stripped of his energy and has to undertake his first regeneration.

2 'The Moonbase' by Kit Pedler (1967)
Location: The Moon.
Contingent: Four Cybermen from their later base on the planet Telos. Clearly much further evolved than the originals. (Actors: John Wills, Peter Greene, Reg Whitehead, Keith Goodman. Voices: Peter Hawkins.)
Operation and Outcome: To take control of the Gravitron, a gravity machine on the Moon, and use it to alter Earth's weather to such a degree that it destroys the planet. Learning that the Cybermen are affected by changes in gravity, the Doctor uses the machine to hurl them and their ships into space.

3 'The Tomb of the Cybermen' by Kit Pedler and Gerry Davis (1967)
Location: Planet Telos.
Contingent: Nine Cybermen, further evolved technologically as evidenced by their creation of the Cybermats. (Actors: Michael Kilgarrit, Hans Le Vries, Tony Harwood, John Hogan, Richard Kerley, Ronald Lee, Charles Pemberton, Kenneth Seeger, Reg Whitehead. Voices: Peter Hawkins.)
Operation and Outcome: A crazed archaeological explorer named Klieg revives what are believed to be the last Cybermen from their tomb on Telos. In order to prevent a further wave of Cyber-terrors, the Doctor freezes the

The Cybermen emerge from the sewers to take over London in the classic story 'The Invasion'

machine-men and also neutralises their mechanical helpers, the Cybermats.

4 'The Wheel in Space' by David Whitaker and Kit Pedler (1968)
Location: Space Station.
Contingent: Two Cybermen, now vastly improved in their invasion techniques. (Actors: Jerry Holmes, Gordon Stothard. Voices: Peter Hawkins and Roy Skelton.)
Operation and Outcome: The Cybermen have infiltrated Cybermats on board the Wheel in Space, a giant space station, with the intention of taking it over and using it as the starting point for an invasion of Earth. Discovering the Cybermats, the Doctor is able to destroy the Cybermen's invasion fleet with the aid of a long-range laser beam – despite the added peril of a meteorite storm.

5 'The Invasion' by Derrick Sherwin & Kit Pedler (1968)
Location: London.
Contingent: Six Cybermen in much changed appearance, complete with zipper below the neck. (Actors: Reg Whitehead, Greg Palmer, Pat Gorman, Harry Brooks, John Wills, Tony Harwood.)
Operation and Outcome: The Cybermen have gained control of a ruthless electronics tycoon, Tobias Vaughn, and are using his products to emit a Cyber-signal which will summon their invasion fleet. Learning of their plan, the Doctor recruits help from the newly-formed UNIT organisation, and though the Cybermen at first gain a foothold through the city's sewers, their plan is defeated when a missile fired at the dark side of the Moon destroys their paralysing weapon.

6 'Revenge of the Cybermen' by Gerry Davis (1975)
Location: Space Station Nerva.
Contingent: Cyberleader and Cybermen who are exposed like all their kind to be vulnerable to gold. (Actors: Christopher Robbie, Melville Jones.)
Operation and Outcome: Another attempt to take over a space station using the Cybermats as a

The original Cybermen as they appeared in 'The Tenth Planet'

forward invasion party. The fourth Doctor uses gold dust to put paid to the Cybermen's plans and at the same time help free the Vogans who have also been much terrorised by the Cybermen.

7 'Earthshock' by Eric Saward (1982)
Location: Earth.
Contingent: Eight – Cyberleader, Cyberlieutenant, and Cybermen, in newly-sophisticated outfits representing still further development. (Actors: David Banks, Mark Hardy, Jeff Wayne, Graham Cole, Peter Gales-Fleming, Steve Ismay, Norman Bradley, Michael Gordon-Brane.
Operation and Outcome: An almost successful operation for the Cybermen who trigger an explosion which is indirectly responsible for the death of the dinosaurs – and also causes the death of the fifth Doctor's companion, Adric. The Doctor can only disperse the Cybermen, rather than defeat them.

8 'The Five Doctors' by Terrance Dicks (1983)
Location: Earth.
Contingent: Three – Cyberleader, Cyberlieutenant, and Cyberscout. (Actors: David Banks, Mark Hardy, William Kenton.)
Operation and Outcome: In his attempts to gain immortality, Lord President Borusa, the Doctor's former teacher at the Time Lord Academy, uses the Time Scoop to bring the Doctor and his previous incarnations to the Death Zone on Gallifrey. Also kidnapped are several squads of Cybermen who threaten the first, third and fifth Doctors.

9 'Attack of the Cybermen' by Paula Moore (1984)
Location: Earth, Telos.
Contingent: Four – Cybercontroller, Cyberleader, Cyberlieutenant and Cyberman, in their most advanced outfits to date. (Actors: Michael Kilgarriff, David Banks, Brian Orrell, John Ainley.)
Operation and Outcome: The sixth and latest Doctor finds himself trying to solve the riddle of Halley's Comet and its relevance to the Cybermen's latest plans. With the help of the Cryon women, the Doctor defeats his old enemies once more. But how long before they will appear again?

THE ELUSIVE
COSMOTRAMP

PATRICK TROUGHTON, *the second Doctor, was an elusive figure during the three years he played the role from 1966 to 1969. One journalist, Kenneth Bailey of* The People, *described him as, 'the great unknown, invisible, ungettable, unspeakable-to, forever avoiding the limelight.' Fellow actors who encountered him almost anonymous in crumpled jeans, roomy sweater and old suede shoes, nonetheless found him unforgettable to act with. 'He completely loses his personality in a part,' said one. 'Off the set, he's not even aware of what he's just done physically on it.' Patrick was, in fact, one of the pioneer television character actors in this country, and by the time he came to take on the role of the Doctor had dozens of successful TV appearances behind him ranging from the Disciple Paul of Tarsus, to Charles Dickens' Uriah Heep and even Adolf Hitler! Here he explains the reasons for his elusive attitude and how* Doctor Who *changed his life . . .*

JOHN   WITCHER

THE MAIN REASON I have avoided interviews is because it's like a conjuror telling you how he does his tricks. If you are a character actor – and that is how I see myself – then you need to remain anonymous as a person.

The ideal situation is to play a part and then go out on the street and nobody knows it was you. If you go around promoting yourself then you are defeating the very thing you are trying to achieve as a character actor – to be unknown as a person and only emerge as somebody on the screen.

The reason for my reticence is really just as simple as that. But now that *Doctor Who* has become such a big success, I don't mind talking about the part. As long as I don't have to do it too often!

My association with *Doctor Who* actually began in Ireland. I was there in 1966 filming *The Viking Queen* with Nicola Pagett when the phone started ringing. It was the BBC production office and they were looking for a replacement for Billy Hartnell, who was then a very sick man.

'Come and play Doctor Who,' the voice on the phone said.

'No, no,' I said equally emphatically, 'I don't *want* to play Doctor Who.'

Anyway, the phone kept on ringing and I kept on saying, 'No, I *really* don't want to play it. It wouldn't last more than six weeks with me!'

But still they kept on phoning and pushing the money up, so that in the end I began to have serious doubts. Well, you see, I *had* watched *Doctor Who* with the family ever since it had started, and *they* all loved it. But I still felt that maybe after three years it had gone on long enough. Perhaps, though, I thought, it was *me* that was wrong?

After about a week of these calls, I decided I must be crazy to keep refusing. It was just ridiculous. Even if it only lasted six weeks it was still worth doing.

So I finally told them, 'OK, I'll do it,' telling myself at the same time that perhaps after a couple of episodes they would still finish with it. Even so, I encouraged myself by thinking that it would have been just another job and I could forget it and move on to the next.

Overleaf: The second Doctor (Patrick Troughton) and Jamie (Fraser Hines) enjoy a joke on the set of 'The Invasion'

IAIN GARDNER

He knew that I had a penchant for comedy, and I sensed immediately what he was after. And so we went to the costumers, and sorted out a whole lot of ragged stuff – after the style of Billy Hartnell, but Billy Hartnell as a tramp.

There was also another element to be considered. Because my children were fans of the programme – my daughter was then about twelve, and my sons ten and eight – I obviously had them at the back of my mind and tailored the role to their likes and dislikes. Perhaps if I had had a grown-up family it might have been a different character altogether that emerged. But with my children being young I didn't want to make the character too frightening for boys and girls.

Mind you, I have never thought the horror elements in *Doctor Who* have been harmful to children. I think it's far worse in the cinema. There it's dark and a child is not in contact with his or her family.

I remember as a child myself I used to hide under the seat at things like *The Invisible Man*. But when you're at home – the lights are on, you're with your family and there's a convenient sofa to hide behind. That's all right – that's *fantasy*.

If there was an element of the uncertain in the way I played the Doctor, it was the fact that no-one could be sure whether I would ever get things right. That apparently frightened children more than anything. They had no faith that I was going to solve the mystery in the end – although, of course, we always did!

When I started playing the role I decided it was important to create a real contrast to Billy Hartnell's interpretation, and to begin with I went a bit over the top. I think I shocked some of the people and there were some things that had to be toned down.

Part of this toning down came in the shape of the comic element which I introduced. A lot of the jokes were things we put in as we went along.

I remember that Frazer Hines and I had this down to a fine art. At the final run-through before filming we would put in things we knew wouldn't be accepted and at the same time slipping in things that probably wouldn't be seen or noticed. This way the more obvious jokes would be thrown out and the more subtle ones retained.

Little did I know! Here I am talking about the role over fifteen years later, and *Doctor Who* is still going strong.

I had several ideas about how to play the Doctor when we started. I thought, 'I know, I'll be like Conrad Veidt in *The Thief of Bagdad*.' I could wear black make-up, huge ear-rings and a turban, and then if the series flopped I could clean up my face and nobody would know I had even done it! That idea didn't go down well, though.

Another idea was to play him as a very tough Victorian windjammer captain complete with naval peaked cap and brass buttons. I even dressed up in this rig to show Sydney Newman, but he took one look and shook his head.

'No, no, Pat,' he said. 'What I want is a sort of Chaplinesque character. A kind of tramp. A cosmic hobo!'

Opposite: The second Doctor, Zoe (Wendy Padbury) and a strangely altered Jamie (Hamish Wilson) face a clockwork soldier in 'The Mind Robber'

Another dodge that we had if we thought the script was too long, was to read it through very slowly at rehearsal. This way the lady with the stopwatch who timed everything would say the script was too long and lines would be cut. That way we didn't have so much to learn!

Of course a story could always be padded out with action if necessary!

Frazer once put me in my place when I complained, 'I've got all these lines to say and all you brats have to do is ask me, "Why?" and perhaps "When?"'

He said straight away, 'You're being paid to say them. Debbie is being paid to get the Dads in from the garden and I'm paid to keep the girls from doing their knitting!'

We were always playing jokes when making Doctor Who. Both Debbie Watling and Wendy Padbury suffered from the pranks Frazer and I

pulled. They were so easy to tease!

I remember standing in the TARDIS on one occasion with Frazer and Debbie, waiting for our cue to step out into the studio. Just before we got the cue, Frazer looked at me, winked, and nodded at Debbie who was composing herself.

I knew exactly what he had in mind. As one we grabbed her pants and whipped them down. And there she was giggling away, trying to struggle back into her pants as the cue came to go on! I don't know if that's printable, but some of the things we got up to were certainly pretty bawdy!

At the end of three years I knew I had had enough. It's not too long, so that you're typecast – and we do all have to make a living for the rest of our lives.

Otherwise, if you stay too long you go into something new and everyone says, 'Oh, it's Doctor Who.' And that's no good. You must try and get them to forget – hoodwink them into forgetting. And that *is* possible.

My time as the Doctor was one of the happiest periods of my life and I was very pleased to return in both 'The Three Doctors', 'The Five Doctors', and most recently 'The Two Doctors'.

'The Five Doctors' was wonderful and I fell right back into the part at once. The only thing I regret is not getting the hair right. My make-up lady, fifteen years earlier, used to lift it with curlers, so it was fairly high on my head. This time I forgot, so that although the length was right it didn't look the same. It was my own hair, though, and not a wig, though perhaps it looked like one!

I wouldn't mind appearing in *Doctor Who* again, either. It would be nice to remake 'Evil of the Daleks', which was a classic, as a full-length feature film. It probably wouldn't break all box office records, but in this day of videos I am sure there would be a ready market.

Most of all I'd love to sneak back in a cameo part disguised as one of the monsters. It would have to be without anyone knowing and with no credit in the *Radio Times*.

But just imagine – the Doctor as a Yeti or even a Cyberman!

Opposite: The second Doctor and Jamie on location for 'The Invasion'

TIMOTHY S. KEABLE

THE TECHNOLOGICAL TIMES

BARRY LETTS, one of the most experienced BBC producers, was the man who supervised the advent of Doctor Who into colour as well as the introduction of several major new technological processes into the production. As a man with a passionate interest in new inventions, he was also ideally suited to handle radical changes in the format and direction of the series. A former actor in the early days of television (he worked with Patrick Troughton in several productions), Barry is also a talented writer and director, and in the following pages talks about his landmark era in Doctor Who . . .

A. KERR

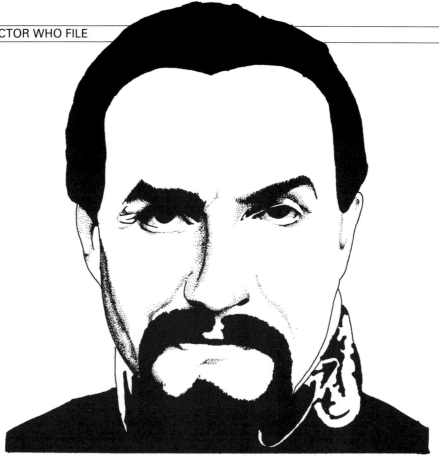

WAS LUCKY in that my taking over as producer of *Doctor Who* coincided with the introduction of colour to BBC 1. This opened up whole new areas of technology and we were actively encouraged to experiment with them.

However, to appreciate the changes that were made during my time as the producer of the series, you have to understand what it was like making the programme before.

When I undertook my first assignment for the series as director of Pat Troughton in 'Enemy of the World' in 1967, the length of the season was about forty weeks of the year. The episodes were recorded one day a week, with five days of outside rehearsal beforehand – so the cast and crew were on a treadmill with very little time to catch their breath.

The director and his team, of course, would only be concerned with one story – perhaps of six episodes – but even this was quite exhausting, entailing up to sixteen hours work a day, seven days a week. And as for the regulars in the cast, they were so busy that very often they couldn't even be spared for location filming. This had to be done with doubles – at least for long shots!

The original Master as played by the late Roger Delgado in 'The Sea Devils'

I remember, for example, that the wife of our production manager, Martin Lisemore – who was later to become famous as the producer of *I, Claudius* and other classic serials – doubled for Deborah Watling in 'Enemy of the World'. Just try and spot her, though!

The schedule for a show which had become as complicated as *Doctor Who* was then very nearly impossible. Rehearsing for four or five days, having one day's camera rehearsal, culminating in an hour and a quarter recording session made incredible demands not only on the actors and directors, but also on the designer, costume and make-up.

This, then, was the situation when I took over as producer. I inherited the planning of the first Jon Pertwee season from my predecessors, Peter Bryant and Derrick Sherwin. They had completed the first 'new look' story, 'Spearhead from Space', which had been made all on film and on location. This was followed by 'The Silurians' and 'Ambassadors of Death'.

The first story in which I was completely

involved from conception was 'Inferno', and with it I was able to try an idea which had been nagging at me for some time. Instead of doing one episode a week, we did two a fortnight.

That may sound the same, but it isn't. The cast would rehearse with the director in the outside rehearsal room two episodes concurrently for the whole of the first week and most of the second, having two days' camera rehearsal in the studio and a two and a half hour recording on the second day.

There were enormous advantages in this approach. The sets only had to be put up and struck once in two weeks instead of twice. The cast had time to learn their lines and let their characters grow. Everybody had time to *think*.

Having started to change the schedule, we gently pushed for more and more facilities, particularly in the actual amount of recording time. The producers who came after me continued the process, until nowadays when a four part serial has over thirty hours of recording time, plus extra days devoted solely to special effects.

The *Doctor Who* programme was, in fact, in the forefront of the development of Colour Separation Overlay, otherwise known as CSO or Chromakey. Basically, CSO is used to combine two pictures to achieve a third. For example, one camera shoots a picture of an actor against a plain-coloured background – usually blue, though green, red or yellow are sometimes used. Wherever the camera 'sees' blue, the CSO apparatus will replace it with the output of another camera, which becomes the background in the final picture. As a result the actor can be put into any setting you like, even a model. And by moving the first camera, the actor can be made to 'float' as did the Super-Being in the last episode of 'The Mutants' made in 1972.

We used CSO a lot in 'The Ambassadors of Death'. The monitor screen in Space Control, the interior of the alien space ship, and even the strange skin colouration of the alien ambassador were all achieved by using CSO.

Indeed, the whole of that first season was very experimental, though I was not too happy with it from another point of view. Apart from 'Spearhead From Space', all the stories were in seven episodes. Now in budget terms, that was fine, for the most expensive episodes of a serial can be said to be the first when one has new sets,

new costumes and new monsters. So the fewer 'first nights' the better.

But seven episodes is really too long for a *Doctor Who* story. There is a grave danger of episodes five and six being just padding. The ideal length is four episodes.

I have special memories of 'Terror of the Autons' which Bob Holmes wrote and I directed in 1971. Having been a director for some years, I wanted to keep my hand in by swopping my producer's hat for that of the director from time to time. What a story to have chosen!

This was the story which introduced Roger Delgado as the Master. Very early in the planning of that particular series, my Script Editor, Terrance Dicks, and I had talked of giving the Doctor a 'Moriarty' – like Sherlock Holmes's perpetual adversary.

As soon as we had thought of the character I knew who I wanted to play it. I'd known Roger for many years. I remember having a great sword fight with him in the surf near Hastings in a costume drama we appeared in together. He had the enormous capacity for villainy – and charm – that the part of the Master demanded.

Looking back, I must admit that we overdid the Master in his first year. He was the main villain in every single story. And after a while the audience twigged this and started looking for him. So in later seasons we restricted him to one or two appearances.

'Terror of the Autons' also got us into quite a lot of trouble. The Auton mannikins, for one thing, had the power to bring plastic to life. And there was also a plastic doll that killed people.

Almost immediately we had letters telling us of children who were afraid to take their teddy bears to bed in case they came alive and strangled them. And there was also a pained letter from Scotland Yard complaining that our plastic killer policemen were undoing all their efforts to persuade children to see the local constable as a friend.

Though we went too far on this occasion, I was always very keen to relate the stories to reality. Before Jon Pertwee's era, the majority of *Doctor Who* stories fell into the category of science-fantasy rather than science-fiction. I am convinced that the best stories have a wild

Opposite: Patrick Troughton as Salamander in 'Enemy of the World' directed by Barry Letts

science-fiction idea related strongly to everyday life.

Of course, we were helped by being able to set many of our stories on present-day Earth. After a while, though, it became ridiculous that so many different alien life forms wanted to take over our planet – so we gradually restored the Doctor's freedom of travel in the TARDIS, beginning with 'Colony in Space'.

There is a funny story connected with that serial set on a bleak Earth-like planet populated by colonists and the unscrupulous members of the Interplanetary Mining Corporation. Viewers may recall that the IMC first officer was a very thinly disguised brutal killer, despite his smart black uniform.

Now we thought it would be a good idea to change that character slightly and make it a woman rather than a man. After all women in Doctor Who tended to be there for one reason only: to scream at the monsters. So it seemed a good excuse to have a really evil villainess.

We cast Susan Jameson in the role and this was even publicised in one of the newspapers. Then, one morning, I got a phone call from my head of department. Apparently he had read the scripts and was afraid that the public might find the notion of a female killer in a black, jack-booted uniform rather 'kinky' – and so I was asked to change the role back to a male!

Several of the Doctor Who stories were inspired by interests of mine. For instance, 'The Green Death' (1973), which Robert Sloman wrote, came about after Terrance Dicks and I had read a series of pieces in an environmental magazine about the pollution of the Earth by man. The articles were very disturbing and made me wish I could do something positive about it.

Terrance and I were talking about this and he said, 'One of the things we could do is produce a Doctor Who story about pollution and get people thinking about it.'

So, that was exactly what we did.

'Planet of the Spiders' (1974) which Robert Sloman also wrote came about for two reasons. I am a Buddhist (though I dislike such labels) and, although not many people realised it at the time, the Spiders' story was a parable about Buddhist meditation.

Sometimes greed can take over the selfish Ego and can use the mind to gain power, rather than

allow itself to be destroyed – which is the point of meditation. In 'Planet of the Spiders', the Great One represented this Ego. However, the Doctor by going into the depth of the Blue Mountain (i.e. into his own self) was the means of destroying the Ego and in the process was transformed into the 'new man' – that is, Tom Baker!

The second origin of that story was Jon Pertwee's interest in gadgetry and my own fascination with super-technology and invention. Jon had already acquired, out of his own pocket, the Whomobile and during the preparations for his last season, he asked me to go along with him to the Boat Show at Earl's Court. He'd been there earlier and spotted on one of the stands a miniature hovercraft which could travel on land or water. Jon wondered if we could use the boat in Doctor Who – and it seemed like a good idea.

The trouble was, all through the season we had been promising Jon the use of auto-gyros, speed boats, and other fast modes of transport in the programme, and I suddenly realised that we were getting perilously near the end of the season and the promise had not been kept.

So for 'Planet of the Spiders' we got together all this equipment, chose the locations, and used one of the early episodes as an excuse for a big chase sequence. It was immense fun and I enjoyed directing it!

A lot of people have asked me over the years how we came to do 'The Three Doctors' in 1972. But if you think about it for a moment, it's the most obvious plot device of all. To have a serial where all three of them come together. In fact while I was producer of Doctor Who, hardly a week went by without somebody coming up to me and suggesting this idea! So when we actually came to do the story for the anniversary year, it was more a case of bowing to pressure than divine inspiration.

Of course, we were very lucky in doing the story when we did as Bill Hartnell sadly died a couple of years later. Pat Troughton was keen on the idea, too, when he heard it, and I was very pleased to work with him again. He and I had actually been working together in one way or another since 1950 when he played Guy Fawkes and I was one of the conspirators!

I think we did change the face of Doctor Who quite dramatically over the period when Jon Pertwee was the Doctor. Certainly, we attracted

BARRY PIGGOTT

a much older age group to the show. We also pushed the technology of the BBC to its limits and, I think, introduced quite a few new elements into the stories. And, perhaps most of all, we all found it immensely rewarding and *fun*!

CHRIS SENIOR

A DANDY SUIT
AND ACTION ROUTES

JON PERTWEE is probably the most versatile entertainer to have played the Doctor. Once a circus performer, bare-back rider, Wall of Death stuntman, not to mention radio star, cabaret performer and magician, he combined all the elements of his remarkable and energetic character into an enormously successful four years with the series, an era that was notable for its use of technology and high speed vehicles. Jon is not only a born entertainer, but also an amusing writer and has already published the first successful volume of his autobiography entitled Moon Boots and Dinner Suits. In the second volume, which he is now working on, he plans to reminisce on his time in Doctor Who in some detail and is understandably saving the best anecdotes and incidents for that book. However, from some delightful conversations I have had with him over the years, I have recalled some of his amusing reflections on life as the Doctor – reflections that he will no doubt be enlarging upon in his eagerly awaited book . . .

ENJOYED EVERY moment I spent as Doctor Who – perhaps most of all because of the opportunity it gave me for *action*! I loved jumping into anything that moved from the diving bell and hovercrafts in 'The Sea Devils', to speeding around the countryside in Bessie, roaring off in the Whomobile or commanding a space capsule in 'The Ambassadors of Death.' And there was even time for the use of the martial arts and a little conjuring when the occasion arose!

Because the Doctor was Earth-bound when I joined the series it was decided that he should be involved with lots of high speed vehicles, and because this is one of my passions it was an element of the character that I revelled in.

You see, I love motor cycles, speed boats and high speed cars. Remember the Whomobile which I helped to design with two engineers from Nottingham who specialised in sprint cars? The vehicle had a pepped-up engine and I had to lie down to drive it rather like in a Grand Prix racing car. Inside it there was a TV, stereo, a telephone and what we called a 'computer bank'. It was probably the most revolutionary vehicle ever made for the series.

I had one or two hairy moments driving that machine – but curiously I came nearest to real danger in the old roadster, Bessie. It was the day Caroline John had to drive it – and no-one realised until she was roaring across a disused airfield that she had never passed her driving test!

Another element of the series I enjoyed was the stunts. Now I can't take all the credit for these as it was a professional stunt man named Terry Walsh who performed the most difficult ones. He was actually quite like me in height and build and there were times when we were confused for one another.

I particularly remember a certain occasion when my wife, Ingeborg, complained bitterly about a sequence in which the Doctor really had seemed to risk life and limb. She was sure it was me, and I had the utmost difficulty convincing her that it was really Terry!

There were, though, times when I actually argued with Terry or the director about doing a

Problems for the Doctor (Jon Pertwee) and Liz Shaw (Caroline John)

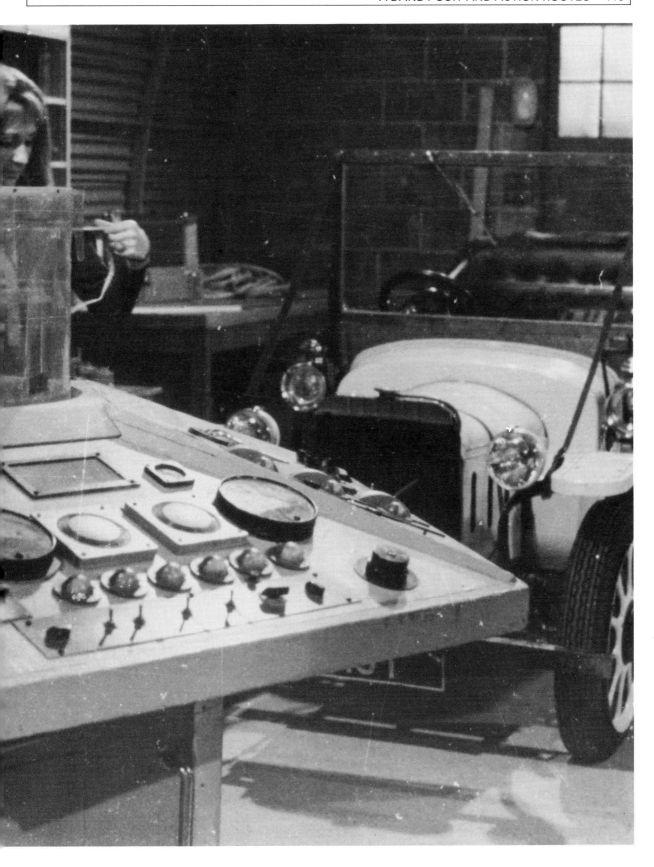

stunt which looked like fun and was not too dangerous.

After one argument – which I won – Terry half glared at me and said, 'All right, you do it – but make it look difficult or I'm out of a job!'

That was the cue for a joke which I would always repeat when Terry had to do something really difficult like fall from a height or take a spill of some kind. 'Hey, Terry!' I would call just as the cameras were about to film, 'Make it look *difficult*!'

On occasions, the bravery of the stuntmen who appeared in *Doctor Who* was amazing. I remember filming a scene for 'Inferno' (1970) in which I had to drive Bessie through a group of raging monsters like primitive apes called Primods. And to add as much realism as possible to the scene it was decided that I should knock one of them over with the car.

Opposite: The Doctor and Liz are confronted by Brigadier Lethbridge-Stewart in 'The Silurians'; *Below:* The Doctor and Liz in Bessie, the Time Lord's beloved motor car

The Primod in question was played by a stunt man called Pat Gorman who told me not to worry and just drive at him as though I seriously intended to knock him over. At the last moment, he said, he would leap aside, making it look as though he had been hit.

Unfortunately, though, the stunt went slightly wrong and I *did* strike Pat, fracturing his ankle. However, like a true professional, he rose to his feet after the incident and played out the rest of his scene as an indestructible creature defying any attempt to harm him!

I have had the odd accident, too. In one scene for *Doctor Who* I just had to disappear out of camera sight as if I had fallen.

The director said, 'Jon, all you need to do is duck your head.'

I wanted it to look more spectacular, though, and decide to make a backward leap. It looked spectacular all right – but I fell badly on the mattress which had been laid out specially and jarred my spine! It kept me off my motorbike for weeks!

I remember, too, that when I first started in the role, my two children, Dariel and Sean, would sit with me to watch it. Sean was always close by my side, and his eyes would dart constantly from the screen to me.

Finally, I asked him what he was doing. 'I'm just making sure you are all right, Papa!'

I think one of the most interesting memories I have of those days was the way the public reacted. For example, I would be out on location in my rather flamboyant dress of frilly shirt, velvet smoking jacket and opera cloak and yet people would still walk by and say quite casually, 'Good morning, Doctor!'

My outfit actually came about quite by accident. I put it together from a selection of my grandfather's old clothes just for a photo session when my announcement as the new Doctor was being made.

When, later, it came to deciding what I was going to wear in the programme I said that I wanted to have a very elegant suit. But no one would hear of it.

'No, no,' they said. 'The other outfit is just terrific.'

I suppose it made me look the dandy after Pat Troughton's clown and William Hartnell's ragbag!

Curiously, though, this seemed to make children very respectful and admiring. Though I wasn't actually keen on playing the Doctor as some kind of scientific wizard, I did try to let everyone assume that I was a genius and capable of tackling any problem.

Children seemed to believe that my Doctor wouldn't fiddle about but face up to any danger there was and protect them from it. They were therefore a bit in awe, and I remember this had an interesting reaction whenever I made public appearances.

Normally, with crowds of thousands of people you need police control – but this just wasn't necessary. For as I walked through the people, they would just part like the waters of the Red Sea! It was amazing!

Mind you, when I later made appearances as the scarecrow Worzel Gummidge it was quite different. Everyone seemed to want to grab me and I really did need the help of the police!

During my time as the Doctor I was a great believer in bringing the aliens and monsters down to Earth. I always feel there's nothing

more alarming than coming home to find a Yeti in your bathroom! OK, you might expect that in the Himalayas, but not in the average suburb.

In other words, if you saw Daleks exterminating on Westminster Bridge it is so much more frightening than seeing them in outer space.

In fact, I had very little time for the Daleks. It wasn't that I was scared of them – just bored! I thought they had been around too long. And anyway, you only had to run up or down a flight of stairs and they were stuck!

I much preferred the monsters with some life

The Doctor enters into an uneasy deal with the Daleks in 'Death to the Daleks'

in them like the Ogrons and the Draconians. Though most of all I preferred the special effects sequences which were much more alarming than some rubberoid or wooden monster. I'm not sure the children liked them – but I certainly did!

People have asked me since I left the programme whether I think the recent achievements in space have deprived the series of some of its appeal. If anything, I think they have given it more appeal. They've stimulated imaginations.

Just because we have discovered the Moon is uninhabited, it doesn't mean there aren't life forms on other planets of a kind we cannot even conceive. I'm not a great science-fiction person, but I am inclined to believe in UFO's or Flying Saucers. My only real problem, though, is, if they exist, *why* won't the blighters land?

THE MAKER OF MONSTERS

JOHN FRIEDLANDER has an enduring reputation among long-time fans of Doctor Who as the man who created some of the programme's most famous monsters. Although he cannot lay claim to either of the show's top two 'creatures-you-love-to-hate', the Daleks and Cybermen, he was responsible for three of the others voted by viewers into the Top Five Monsters – the Ice Warriors, Sontarans and Zygons. Not to mention the Ogrons, Draconians, Sea Devils, Wirrn, Mummies and the infamous creator of the Daleks, Davros. During his time with the programme, which spanned the Troughton, Pertwee and Tom Baker eras, he played a major part in devising many of the monsters which were as much an appeal for many viewers as the Doctor himself! Yet rarely was he credited for his creatures which, with their moving eyes and mouths as well as special skin texture, had a genuinely realistic and alien look. Here the record is put straight in John's own words . . .

DURING THE years that I was effects designer on *Doctor Who* I used to get quite a lot of fan mail from people saying how much they liked my monsters and hoping that I was going to make still more horrible ones in the future.

It was always very satisfying to know that the audience appreciated your work, although, as I am a bad correspondent, I found it difficult to keep up with those who asked questions about the more gruesome creations. One day, though, I got a letter which almost set *my* hair on end.

It was from an elderly gentleman living in Leeds who told me he was trying to trace his family tree. He said that his name was also Friedlander and he wondered if I knew anything about the history of the name.

Enclosed with the letter was a drawing of the family tree which went as far back as he could trace. It appeared at first glance as if we might belong to the same branch of the family. But something else really brought me up short. For my correspondent had discovered that a certain Miss Friedlander had years ago married one Baron Von Frankenstein!

After my initial surprise, I couldn't help laughing. Baron Von Frankenstein, the great monster maker, married to a Friedlander! A case of monsters to monsters!

Curiously, I have always seemed to get involved with the Grand Guignol type of programme and end up producing dead bodies, decapitated heads and cut-off hands. It is a fact, though, that I always wanted to be a sculptor, and at college I studied sculpture and stained glass work.

For a while I worked in advertising designing little display sculptures and animated models for department stores. Then in 1960 I joined the BBC Visual Effects Department and became the first visual effects sculptor. I remember there were six of us in a workshop so small that it was only possible for two people to work at a time – the others had to watch!

I worked on *Doctor Who* from the early days and mostly made masks and other small sculptures. One of my first major jobs was for the Pat Troughton story, 'The Seeds of Death' (1969), in which I made the half-mask for Slaar, the leader of the Ice Warriors, played by Alan Bennion. The appliance was a thin layer of latex rubber fashioned to look reptilian in nature which fitted the actor's features perfectly and ran from his nose, over his mouth and around his neck.

My first set of full masks was for the ape-like beings, the Ogrons, who appeared in 'Day of the Daleks' in 1972. Originally, they were going to be actors made up, but it seemed to me that, as this would take hours, the quickest thing would be to make masks. And so with the aid of some make-up girls who I was instructing at the time in the art of making models, I devised the Ogron mask and they presented a dozen of them to the director as a *fait accompli*. He decided to go ahead and use them. But there were problems, though.

Some of the Ogron actors were such big men – really enormous – that the masks didn't fit. In some cases we had to split them and stick pieces in just to make them fit. It was terrible – but we did learn some valuable lessons.

Making a really successful mask or head, in fact, calls for close collaboration with a lot of people. The first thing I would do would be to have a conference with the writer of the story and get some idea of what he had in mind. Then the director and producer for their thoughts, and finally make-up and wardrobe departments.

The close-fitting face mask, as opposed to the type of monster head that just slips over the actor's head, is nearly always modelled to the face of the actor who's going to wear it. That way you get a perfect fit – but it also allows you to keep some of the actor's basic features in and get a more 'believable' look.

I start by taking a face-cast, which is a plaster mould of the actor's face. I vaseline his face, sticking the eyebrows down with extra vaseline, and then cover it in plaster bandages. These have to be dipped in hot water and smoothed onto the face, building up to two or three layers. They set in about five minutes and can then be lifted off.

This cast can be removed like a mask, and in fact is light enough to ease off by asking the actor to just blow onto the inside to separate it from his face. This leaves you a hollow

Opposite: A Sea Devil and one of John Friedlander's most memorable creations

impression of the face which you can stiffen up with ordinary plaster on the outside to form the mould.

Then I would press clay into the mould and withdraw it when it was dry so that I had a clay mask of the actor's face. I would build up the back of the head into the shape of the monster because obviously the only part of the actor I wanted was his mouth, his eyes and perhaps his nose.

Now I could start to model my mask around the head – extending his head to the monster shape. When this is complete I take a plaster mould. This is the final mould and I run thin rubber latex solution into it to make the mask. When, later, I pull it out, there is the finished mask for the actor to wear.

Another technique I used was to mix a finely

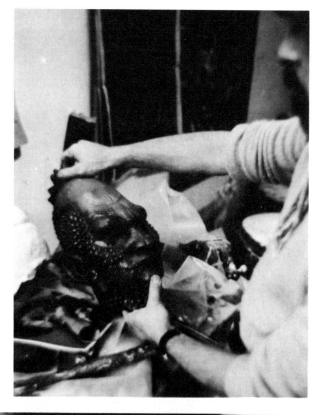

Right and Below: The making of a Draconian mask – based on Dave Allen's head!
Opposite: A Silurian, another of John Friedlander's creations

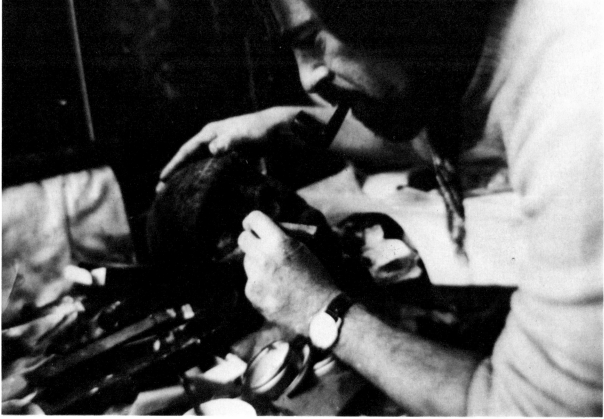

ground silica powder with the latex solution. This made the rubber react like clay so that I could actually model the mask in rubber. The masks for the Draconians who appeared in the Jon Pertwee story, 'Frontier In Space' (1973), were made like this.

There was only a vague description of them in the script. They were supposed to be a dragon-like race of humanoids distinguished by bumps of some kind on their faces. However, until I came up with the design that was eventually seen on television no one was really sure what they wanted. As a matter of interest, I modelled the mask on a sculptured head of the comedian Dave Allen because we just happened to have one in the workshop!

The bumps actually made the masks very comfortable for the Draconian actors to wear, because there was an air pocket under each which meant they didn't adhere too rigidly to the face. I heard later that some of the actors felt so at home in their masks that they kept them on during the lunch and dinner breaks in the BBC Canteen! Yes, I was very proud of those monsters.

Sometimes I was asked to design the basic monster suit as well as the head. I did this with the Sea Devils with their turtle-like heads. The producer wanted the characters to be much taller than humans and so the actual Sea Devil head was worn as a 'hat' on top of the actor's head and they looked out through the necks.

The material for these particular monsters had to be tough enough to survive in the cold waters of the English Channel. I was also worried about the effects of salt water on the mask and so I constructed the heads for the six actors from heavy duty latex which I left curing longer in the mould and which eventually set to a leather-like consistency.

Together with the costume supervisor, I then blended the texture of the mask in with the suit – although in the end I do think everything looked a little out of proportion.

That same year, 1973, I designed the masks for another monster that became very popular with viewers – the Sontarans. In actual fact, I made two masks for the actor Kevin Lindsay who played the Sontaran captain, Linx, in 'The Time Warrior' and Styre, the cruel officer in 'The Sontaran Experiment' (1975).

If you examine photographs from the

programmes you can see that there are differences between the two – Linx's head was very dome-shaped, while Styre had something of the appearance of a gargoyle!

What happened was that Linx's head somehow got lost between the two stories, and so they asked me to make another. I think the second was the better of the two as the mouth was more flexible.

I had a lot of fun making the giant insect-like grubs, the Wirrn, for 'The Ark in Space', Tom Baker's second story in January 1975. They were quite a departure from the sort of monsters we had done up until then. I discovered this polythene packing material filled with bubbles which someone had brought into the studios and I thought it would be ideal for the skin of the grubs. No one had used this kind of material before – though it has been used a lot since – and I thought it worked beautifully.

What made it even more enjoyable was that I got a chance to actually play the grub at the rehearsals! Stuart Fell, the man who was due to play the role on film, wasn't due to be in the studio until the final shooting and so I stepped in and played the grub. I thought my grubs were rather good!

I was also very pleased with the mask of Davros which I made for Michael Wisher in 'Genesis of the Daleks' (1975). I worked on this with Peter Day, the visual effects designer on that show, who made the mobile base and back. I did the complete head and hands, using ordinary latex, and considering that Michael hadn't then been cast and I had to work purely on spec, I think the result was very dramatic.

As a matter of interest, apart from the various substances I have mentioned, I have also used fibre-glass in my work, in particular for the head masks worn by the mummies in 'Pyramids of Mars' (1975).

The Zygons who appeared that same year in 'Terror of the Zygons' were actually a co-creation with the costume designer, Jim Acheson. They were based on a pre-foetus shape and Jim had already done some drawings and plasticine models when I became involved.

The problem was the producer wanted the mask complete with its high-domed forehead and array of suction cups to fit the actor's face, but Jim just wasn't sure how this could be done. I was able to solve the problem by making the

face in rubber and the body in fibre-glass.

First, I had to cast up a full body using clay built over a metal armature because the weight of the clay was such that it would have collapsed without one. I didn't build a complete body, but just the head and a few vital sections of the body.

The second part of the operation was to bond these bits of fibre-glass together with various pieces of rubber to make the final shape. It was a terrible job, as I recall, because we had only a few weeks to get it right!

The Daleks and their Ogron slaves – also monsters from the hands of John Friedlander

Since I left the BBC and became a freelance special effects designer, the weird and bizarre have still continued to come my way. Readers may well recall the Vogans in *The Hitch-Hiker's Guide to the Galaxy* which were my work.

I remain pleased, though, to have been a part of the team that has made *Doctor Who* such a success over the years.

BARRY PIGGOTT

'I had very little time for Daleks';
fortunately in this story the Doctor
only had to face the Claws of Axos...

The third Doctor meets his deadliest foes in their city on Spiridon in this scene from 'Planet of the Daleks'

A disused sandpit serves as an extraterrestrial landscape for a Dalek

Running along metal tracks, the Daleks found themselves temporary uneasy allies with the Doctor and his friends on Exxilon ('Death to the Daleks')

The Daleks and their evil creator Davros, played by Michael Wisher, 'the man in the bathchair'

Time Lord meets Sontaran officer: the third Doctor and Linx (Kevin Lindsay) from 'The Time Warrior'

WHO ON EARTH IS TOM BAKER?

TOM BAKER, the fourth Doctor, played the role for a record seven years and made the programme an international institution; as Nancy Mills of The Guardian wrote in 1979: 'He has turned the Doctor into a cult figure replete with fan clubs and Doctor Who Societies.' This phenomenon was observed by all the newspapers, with William Marshall of The Daily Mirror that same year calling Baker 'the megastar of space and time with a following from the high-peaked Andes to the back streets of Bolton.' Yet, for all this publicity, he still remained something of an enigma, as Daniel Farson wrote in The Sunday Telegraph in 1981: 'Baker is elusive, almost an enigma, arriving and leaving alone, vanishing like Doctor Who in his space-time machine.' The truth of the matter was that underneath his larger-than-life personality and jovial eccentricity, there was a basically shy person, much more at home with his young admirers than adult fans or newspaper reporters. Here he explains both the pleasures and pressures of playing the Doctor, and also offers some insights into just how the character became such an international celebrity . . .

I WAS SIMPLY just one of the actors lucky enough to play Doctor Who. During my years in the role I gave the part all I could – though there is one other thing I would have liked to have given it: a completely new type of companion for the Doctor.

Not another beautiful girl, but a much older actress – even somebody very fat who would wheeze around after the Doctor. Now *that* would have been different! I kept suggesting it – but no one would listen. No doubt there were very good reasons, but the idea still makes me smile!

Let me say right away that I have always felt that *Doctor Who* was a children's programme – watched by children of all ages. The Doctor is, of course, a very moral being, for you know exactly what he is going to do and why. There is very little that is unexpected about him.

That, in fact, is one of the major problems of the role – character development. You see, there is none, because the Doctor is a heroic stereotype who conforms to all the patterns of behaviour you expect him to conform to. His character stays basically the same.

The challenge is to make that character as diverting and interesting as possible. Every time I looked at a new script, I would think, 'How can I vary this?' – but it got harder and harder to keep the character fresh.

Over the years I came to understand what the Doctor could and could not do better than any writer or director who has only one story to worry about. I used to spend a long time checking the scripts and dialogue to make sure they conformed to how the Doctor should be played. If I found any scenes that depicted him as being over-emotional or gratuitously violent then I would argue very strongly for their removal.

In fact, I was always making suggestions of

Below: The fourth Doctor (Tom Baker) and a water-logged K9 at Brighton in 'The Leisure Hive';
Opposite: The Doctor and Sarah Jane Smith (Elisabeth Sladen) on the trail of Sutekh in 'Pyramids of Mars'

TIMOTHY S. KEABLE

one kind or another – maybe a new line of dialogue or varying a situation – and most of the directors were very kind to me. Often we reached a compromise, and though they humoured my extravagances, they also took me seriously and some of my ideas were kept in the series. I appreciated that because it made for a good working relationship.

I particularly don't like to see violence on television – especially the mindless type of violence you always get in American cop series. I always prefer to see the baddies out-witted – I didn't think it is necessary to blow them to kingdom-come.

I never felt we went too far in *Doctor Who* – the problem in a series where good always triumphs over the bad is how to show it in a new way.

Comedy was also an important element. Sometimes it is much more diverting to laugh your villains to destruction. And I don't believe we lost any feeling of tension as a result – because in all comedy there has to be the moments of seriousness and the contrast between the two is very effective.

When I took over the role of the Doctor my brief was to suggest that he was not human and that he should accordingly have mannerisms that were somehow alien to those around him.

For my part I came to believe that the Doctor should have an air of naive innocence about him

to counter his enormous wealth of knowledge and past experience. He had to seem vulnerable and therefore more interesting to an audience I felt would quickly tire of the Doctor as Superman!

My basic approach to new situations was to walk boldly into them and say with a broad grin, 'Hello, I am the Doctor.' Now the audience may be aware, from previous scenes, that the Doctor is going into a situation of dire peril, but their attention is held, subconsciously knowing that, any second now, he is going to get knocked to the floor!

Playing the part also put special demands on me. For I was not only the Doctor on the screen, I had to live out this idea of a semi-perfect man in my own life. It was another reason that made – and still makes – the series unique.

All those years I had to be aware that I had virtually no existence as Tom Baker. Apart from a few close friends and colleagues, everybody else called me the Doctor. I was aware that they were not looking at me but at the image they had of this character.

It was important to me, therefore, that I never disappointed people, especially children. I could

Opposite: The yo-yo goes up and down in time; the Doctor goes in and out of time

CHRIS SENIOR

never be seen being raucous in the streets, or plastered, or smoking cigars.

When I did want to go out for some fun, I had to do it discreetly in selected actors' bars or clubs. Even then there was sometimes no escape. I remember a friend once took me to a very select West End club. 'Don't worry,' he said, 'we won't be bothered here.' Well, we had not been there more than a few minutes when a chap raised his glass and said, 'My dear Doctor. How nice to see you!' I remember how astonished my friend was. For the man was a High Court judge!

I never wanted children to be disillusioned. I believed that if they saw me behaving badly they would lose that sense of magic about the Doctor.

Even if I was feeling slightly depressed I was still obliged to turn on a performance when I met anyone to show that I was coping and life was very sweet. That was never too hard with children – I have always got on well with them – it was when adults wanted me to do it that I found it so tiresome.

You see, unlike children who were just watching the Doctor, adults were looking at Tom Baker playing the Doctor and so when they saw me in person they often used me as a springboard to voice their protests about certain aspects of the programme as though it was my fault for playing the Doctor in a way that did not appeal to them. It could be *very* tedious!

Some of my chums used to tease me about my attitude to the role and thought it was all a bit unnecessary, but then they didn't have my sense of responsibility to the image of the show. I know some people might think that very pompous, but it was something I had thought very long and carefully about.

Mind you, being on your best behaviour can be very, very exhausting! And it's not helped by the press who are always looking for a bit of gossip about someone like me.

Becoming the Doctor changed my life, of course, and when I accepted the part I dreaded being asked how I was going to play it. In fact, I didn't really know, and if you look back to those early episodes and see a certain air of spontaneity in them, it was because I really didn't know what was happening a lot of the time!

Following Jon was a daunting task, too. He had been playing the part for five years and I thought that to everyone he was the Doctor. He had been well known before he joined the series, whereas nobody had heard of me. In hindsight, I think it was a very brave decision to cast me.

What I didn't know then – but have come to appreciate since – is that any good actor playing the Doctor cannot fail, because the show has gone past this point. It can continue in spite, and because of, the actor playing the lead.

Because I never watched the series I find it difficult to remember specific stories that pleased me. I do, though, remember that we had some excellent villains and extraordinary monsters. Some of them were so *funny*.

There was a regular cast of actors who played these monsters and we all became great friends. There were the giant, man-eating plants, the Krynoids, in 'The Seeds of Doom', in which Tony Beckley gave such a fine performance. And I also liked the Wirrn and that giant rat in 'The Talons of Weng-Chiang' which looked so good.

Whenever I encountered a new monster, however, I couldn't be frightened, and I had to say something like, 'Hello, what are you?' I'd immediately get knocked out for my pains, and as soon as I came round would have to remark ruefully, 'Well, we'd better look out for *him* in future!'

My aim was always for the Doctor to be in a state of delight and anticipation about whatever was going on – and that even included danger!

[Editor's Note: As part of the BBC's promotion for the Tom Baker era as the Doctor, a 'What's What' of his favourite monsters was prepared and this is published later in the book.]

K9 was also a bit of a monster, especially to act with. We had tremendous technical problems with that dog and it was always breaking down. This invariably happened when we were on location and caused just the kind of hold-ups you don't need when you are on such a tight schedule.

Many of the villains were quite frightening – I used to try to believe in them so as to communicate the threat they presented to the audience. In some cases that wasn't too difficult because they were so convincing.

I would like to have had more historical adventures meeting real people. For instance, it would have been very interesting for the Doctor to have met Izaak Walton and talked about fishing, or Isaac Newton and talked about

gravity. Just imagine, the Doctor could have told Newton he had got it all wrong and proved it to him! Of course, it would have been so far outside Newton's experience that he would have had him thrown out of his house!

I'm also surprised that no-one the Doctor ever met commented on his bizarre appearance. Or that having helped someone, they did not show appreciation by copying his attire. I could have had an army all dressed like me – and all tripping over their scarves! Mind you, when I attend conventions these days I do often find myself face to face with people dressed just as I was!

I also wish that I could have made the full-length feature film, *Doctor Who Meets Scratchman* which I devised with Ian Marter. The script was very frightening but had lots of humour and I thought it would make a brilliant film. But we just couldn't raise enough enthusiasm and money. [Editor's Note: Ian Marter explains the background to this fascinating project later in the book.]

I also enjoyed writing a weekly column for *Reveille*, because it gave me a chance to communicate with my audience – a typical column is reprinted here – and I was once offered a substantial sum to write a book about the making of *Doctor Who*. Now, I love books and reading, but somehow, once I had decided to leave, I wanted to make it final. It was a hard decision, for I owe a great deal to the show.

Having played a fantastic, larger-than-life character, I'm interested in playing more of them. I love people like Captain Hook or Long John Silver. Even Chekhov – Uncle Vanya's not a hundred miles from the Doctor, though some would take issue with that. What I do know is that I could not stop being an actor. That's all I am.

The Doctor worries over an unconscious Sarah Jane in 'The Hand of Fear'

THE DOUBLE LIFE OF DOCTOR WHO

As Tom Baker mentioned, in 1975 he wrote a weekly column for the now defunct newspaper, Reveille, and in it he aired his views on a variety of topics from botany to book collecting as well as using it as a means of communicating with the huge army of fans who literally deluged him with mail. The column, 'Doctor Who Writes For You', lasted for over a year and delighted readers of all ages. Here is a typical column from March 1975 spiced with Baker's own brand of humour and pithy remarks . . .

ROBERT SMITH

A S DOCTOR WHO I travel in time and space. Wizard, really! A Time Lord's life is really exciting.

As Doctor Who I have two hearts. That's one of the perks of the job! And as Tom Baker I have two lives.

One is leaving home in the morning to go to work, the same as most adults.

The other is being transformed into someone who finds himself hurtled into all sorts of adventures. Really unearthly ones.

My weird and wonderful time-and-space travellings entertain millions, from the wise men at Pembroke College, Oxford, who record my scientific goings-on, to young people, like the girls who've written to me from Sidcup and South Wales.

You see, in our world, *Doctor Who* is really universal. With no age barriers to restrict his fans, either.

I get letters from mums and dads as well as schoolgirls and boys and that's really super!

Doctor Who is an insatiable rebel. With an insatiable curiosity for life and living.

The Doctor in Highland mood as he ponders the secret of Loch Ness in 'Terror of the Zygons'

You may remember he got bored with just being a Time Lord and took the TARDIS to seek adventure.

There's been a bit of fuss about my new face, and the way Doctor Who looks now, with his wide-brimmed hat, eccentric dress and long scarf.

Some of you don't like my face. I'm sorry about that. It's the only one I've got!

There are whole galaxies yet to explore. Thousands of planets and civilisations to meet. Which of us knows what the future – or past? – may bring?

But whatever the encounter, Doctor Who will face it with fortitude.

Now I'll tell you a secret about Tom Baker.

I'm a bit of a child at heart. I love my job. I love being Doctor Who. I love hearing from my fans.

But I can't come to everybody's tea party!

Listen, it's the rush hour. You are on a train or a bus. The weather is bad, the train is crowded – no seats, everybody pushing and looking miserable. You feel angry and depressed.

Ever had that feeling? Of course you have, and so had I until about three months ago.

Now I get on a crowded tube train or bus, and people are jostling for some comfort and sighing loudly because there isn't any and then . . .

'Hello, Tom' and 'Hello, Doctor' and 'How are the Daleks?' or 'I thought you travelled by TARDIS' and always smiles, smiles, smiles, smiles.

I tell you, it's a great pleasure.

And my mail is different, too. Not just buff envelopes containing boring bills, oh no.

Take this example, for instance: 'I'm not feeling very well today so I thought I'd write to you and the Queen.'

Or this one: 'I decided to write to you as I haven't many friends on account of I'm twelve years old and tall for my age. And I'm typing this letter because I've got a sprained arm.'

And from Johanna Knight, aged four, of Ramsgate, Kent: 'I love you and I hope you kill that green monster.'

Another girl called Sasha Johnston asked, 'What do you eat and when?' Well, Sasha, despite being a Time Lord I still like eggs and bacon and I also eat apples. And when? Oh, whenever I feel like it!

Of course there's no problem about where to go in my spare time. This is a typical invitation from a six-year-old called Christine: 'I like your acting very much. Bournemouth is where I live and I enclose my telephone number if you would like to come and stay.'

And as I was writing this down I thought I would call my six-year-old friend in Bournemouth. And I was lucky – it was Christine who answered the telephone!

I can't tell you what fun it was – she seemed very pleased indeed.

On the train the other day two boys came over casually towards me – very casually, and told me they were feeling nervous! It turned out that it was school report night – and one of the boys said that if his report was bad he wouldn't get the new bike his parents had promised him as a reward for a good report.

IAIN GARDNER

I couldn't help feeling a bit sad for him. He seemed so nice and I thought it was too bad that his school report should scare him. If I'd worried about the quality of *my* school reports I'd have had a breakdown!

Sometimes I think there's less to school than meets the eye. I can remember being told that America was first discovered by Columbus in 1492. I actually believed it and I think the teacher did – silly lady! Before old Columbus and his shipmates got to America there was a thriving, happy society of millions of copper-coloured people called Indians.

So it goes on – letters and friends on the trains, tubes, buses and even in shops. Out of the thirteen million fans of Doctor Who I seem to come across a lot and so far everyone has been delightful. So I can't complain.

Very much the image of the bohemian French painter: Tom Baker as the fourth Doctor in a publicity still for 'City of Death', the first 'Doctor Who' story to be filmed abroad

From Paris to E-Space: the Doctor considers his situation on Alzarius ('Full Circle')

The fifth Doctor (Peter Davison) ponders Tegan's navigation skills in 'Castrovalva'

The first five Doctors, plus their second best
friend, in the twentieth anniversary special
'The Five Doctors'

DOCTOR WHO'S WHAT'S WHAT

KNOW YOUR enemy, as they say. Not so easy when he, she or – mostly – it, can take the form of a robot, a giant wasp, a crazed computer, or a walking vegetable the size of Buckingham Palace.

Doctor Who gets to meet all these and many more – and to overcome their varied villainies – and from the jottings in his 500-year diary, we have transcribed the Doctor's own lighthearted comments on just some of the creatures he has encountered in his travels through time and space.

Autons: Plastic mannikins, quick on the draw, sticky on the uptake.
Cybermen: Tricky. Old enemies. Clever, too – allergic to gold dust – makes them unique. Their

Previous page: An Ice Warrior, deadly invader from Mars;
Opposite: Sarah Jane discovers the disembodied hand of Eldrad in 'The Hand of Fear';
Above: Mummies, robots in the service of Sutekh in 'Pyramids of Mars'

mechanical robots, the Cybermats, are another hazard.
Davros: Good scientist, but bent. Preferred inventing Daleks (uninteresting Daleks, but I've met them so often . . .)
Daleks: Most people probably know more about Daleks than they do about me so I won't describe them. All they do is say, 'Ex-ter-min-ate, ex-ter-min-ate!' And to you, too, Dalek baby.
Draconians: A lot of old dragons, but they have a warm side, too. And not their breath!
Hand, Disembodied: A word of warning. Never pick up a disembodied hand. Can't be good, might be bad. In this case it turned into a beautiful woman and then a chap. That's got to be bad.
Ice Warriors: A cold bunch who don't like it when things get hot. It was a bad day when they were first defrosted . . .
Krynoid: Vegetables that follow you and swallow you. Peripatetic pods, even. Flatter myself that I know all about this garden pest. Met them in

'The Seeds of Doom' and recognised them instantly. It helps to be well connected.

K9: Canine. Get it? A computerised dog with an IQ of over 300.

Master, The: A Time Lord, like me. But this fellow countryman of the planet Gallifrey, where I was born, was a black sheep. Wanted to rule the world. Funny about that – so many others I meet have the same ambition. Has survived many reincarnations . . .

Mandragora: Sounds like a mix between a plant and a dragon, but actually something much more sinister. You can't see it but you can feel it working on you. A mysterious force enslaving mankind. Lucky I fixed it, don't you agree?

Morbius: Messy and unpleasant. A brain on the look-out for a head. Nasty with it, as well.

Mummies: One of the nice things about being a Time Lord is that I enjoy biological built-in advantages. Like a respiratory bypass system. A mummy in 'Pyramids of Mars' tried to strangle me, but I switched to overdrive. Very useful in a tight squeeze!

Ogrons: Do the Daleks' dirty work. Look like apes, behave like them. Strong on muscle, weak on brain power. Should go back to the jungle.

Rat, Giant: Very clever these Chinese. A mixed-up Tong character in Victorian times tried to rule the world. One of his mistakes grew ten foot long and inhabited the sewers under London. Nasty, but not nasty enough to outwit me.

Robots: Come in many different guises. Some rampage and are giant-size. Others as in 'Robots of Death' are more humanoid. Most are dumb but some can talk, or have other attributes, just like planet Earth today. Don't much like robots.

Silurians: Slippery customers these. Got a black eye from the Brigadier. Also had trouble with their relatives, the Sea Devils.

Sontarans: Military-like mob who feed on currents – energy that is, not buns. Too strong by half, and too productive by a million – they can reproduce at a million per minute. A real pain in the neck in fact; and it's in the neck – the probic vent, to be exact – where they're vulnerable.

Styggron: I like rhinoceroses. Styggron looks a bit like a rhino gone wrong. I don't like him a bit. He's chief scientist of the Kraals. Don't think much of them either.

Vampires: Real bunch of blood-suckers, believed to be immortal. I had to go for the heart of their leader in the good, old-fashioned way!

Wirrn: Wasps I don't like. But Wirrns, which are wasp-like and seven-foot high, are different. Not cuddly because they eat people. But not all bad either.

Xoanon: Would you believe a schizophrenic computer? If not, why not?

Yeti: Nothing abominable about these snowmen – the real thing are peaceful, shy creatures. But the hostile crowd I encountered were actually robots controlled by the Great Intelligence.

Zygons: There is a monster in Loch Ness and Zygons live off its glandular extract. Let Zygons be Zygons, some people say – I don't. But then, I won!

ALAN ROWLEY

Professor Kettlewell's robot from the fourth Doctor's debut story

THE EPIC
THAT NEVER WAS

IAN MARTER, who played the fourth Doctor's amiable and well-meaning companion, Harry Sullivan, was also a close friend of Tom Baker off the screen, and between them the two men dreamed up the most ambitious full-length film project ever associated with Doctor Who. Ian, who entered acting through the Bristol Old Vic as an assistant stage manager (or 'dogsbody' as he refers to the job), first appeared in the Jon Pertwee era of Doctor Who as Andrews in 'Carnival of Monsters' (1973). Andrews was very much the prototype for Harry Sullivan, originally planned as the fourth Doctor's 'strong arm man'. A close friendship and respect developed between Ian and Tom Baker, and together they planned the cinema movie, Doctor Who Meets Scratchman. Ian, an accomplished writer and now the author of several Doctor Who novelisations (as well as a four-part story for the series which sadly proved impracticable), here recalls the background to this 'epic that never was' and reveals enough of the plot and proposed stars to make any Doctor Who fan scream with anguish that it has not been made . . .

TOM SOUNDED extremely confident. 'Listen, I think we can write a script for ourselves,' he told me one day at the Acton Rehearsal Rooms, 'and I've got an idea for a story.'

I put aside *The Times* crossword we had both been racking our brains over during breaks in rehearsal and listened with mounting enthusiasm as Tom outlined his concept for a *Doctor Who* plot. It involved the Devil and some scarecrows and it sounded marvellous. I was hooked right from the start.

At odd moments during the next few days we

Harry Sullivan (Ian Marter) and Sarah Jane discuss the Cybermen's plans with Tyrum (Kevin Stoney) in 'Revenge of the Cybermen'

then rehearsing. When we had eventually worked out a rough plot Tom took the idea to the Production Office. To our disappointment the reaction was not at all encouraging. So we went back to the drawing board more determined than ever to succeed.

We decided to abandon the idea of a television script. The programme had recently started to figure prominently in the ratings and Tom and I agreed that the time was ripe for a new *Doctor Who* feature film. Two low-budget films had been produced in the Sixties starring Peter Cushing as the Doctor. However, it seemed obvious to us that the actor currently playing the Doctor – Tom himself – should star in any film, rather than a big name totally unconnected with the television show.

In the following weeks Tom and I met from time to time to adapt our scenario to cinematic terms. We wanted to keep the cast small – The Doctor, a male and a female associate and a villain called Scratchman (an ancient name for the Devil) plus a number of minor characters. Our monsters were to be scarecrows and a horde of quasi-cybernetic goblins in Scratchman's pay. We tried to keep the storyline tight, outlawing cheap devices wherever possible – like those familiar scenes where supposedly superintelligent villains armed with spectacular and frightening technology are nevertheless reduced to tying up their human victims or locking them in cupboards in order that later they can conveniently escape or be easily rescued by a hero.

We concentrated on strong visual interest and on fast action. Of course sharp and witty dialogue was vital too, but Tom and I and Lis Sladen had got into the habit, during rehearsals for the programme, of suggesting cuts in our dialogue in favour of images and action, and we wanted to apply this principle in our film script. Naturally a certain amount of verbal exposition was necessary, particularly for the benefit of younger members of the audience. And dumb questions from idiot assistants were out too!

The eccentricity and the Britishness of the television show were deliberately emphasised. The trigger for Tom's plot was an amateur game of cricket played by the Doctor and his friends on a picnic and our climactic final scene neatly tied this up with another game of cricket, this time in celebration of their victory over Evil. But

batted ideas to and fro, developing a storyline for a four-episode *Doctor Who* and jotting our thoughts down on the back of the script we were

was it a victory? Had Scratchman perished or had he escaped? We deliberately made the ending ambiguous so that if the film was a success, then a sequel might be possible!

To boost our morale during one of our frequent bouts of writers' block, Tom arranged for us to see a private showing of the two Peter Cushing *Doctor Who* films. We emerged from the Wardour Street viewing theatre with our spirits raised. We knew we could do a lot better. No disrespect is intended to Mr Cushing, by the way. He is a remarkable actor of great talent and versatility. But the films were a travesty of the *Doctor Who* ethos. They were crude, vulgar and condescending to the audience.

Soon after this, Harry Sullivan was dropped from the series. However, Tom and I continued to meet whenever possible to work on our scenario. Tom brought film director James Hill into the project to collaborate in the preparation of a draft screenplay and to draw up a preliminary budget. We worked as often as our separate commitments allowed at Tom's place or at James's delightful and eccentric house in Shepherds Bush and at last the screenplay was printed and the budget completed.

To reduce production costs, we planned to shoot the film almost entirely on location in Scotland, and probably on Lanzarote in the Canary Islands, where the volcanic wasteland would be ideally suited to the story. There was to be one gigantic finale scene in the studio.

By now we had a script, a budget, a director and an agreement with the BBC assigning us the film rights for two years.

All we needed now was the money!

I was not directly involved in the financial prospecting, but James and Tom worked tirelessly to raise the modest investment our project required. Of course in those days *Doctor Who* had not yet generated the huge and growing following it now enjoys in the United States, so our budget was scaled to recoup costs and hopefully make a profit from its release in the United Kingdom and perhaps countries like Australia where the television show was well known. However, we knew that we could not hope to raise all the capital in the UK. So in addition to the Film Finance Corporation here, approaches were made to organisations like Warner Brothers, Disney, Hammer, Roger Corman, Universal and many others.

James produced a revised and improved version of the screenplay and more approaches were made. Months went by. Hopes were raised, only to be dashed again. We had encouraging reactions from several prospective stars. Vincent Price expressed great interest in the role of Scratchman and Twiggy liked the idea of playing the Doctor's young lady companion. One American mogul in Los Angeles suggested that Doug McClure would be ideal casting for the young man! Eat your heart out, Ian Marter!

But after months of effort and despite the possibility of a promising cast we had only a small proportion of the money in sight. Our optimism began to fade.

And then one day Tom rang to suggest that we go to see the press preview of a new science-fiction blockbuster from America called *Star Wars*. Next day we emerged from the Dominion Cinema into the cold grey wet of Tottenham Court Road feeling utterly dejected. The film we had just seen told us that we were too late. The scale of our project was far too small. Science-fantasy was obviously going to be *in* . . . but on a new and on a vaster scale than ever before. Our project would be a minnow among the whales!

Our problem was not that we were asking for too much money, but that we weren't asking for nearly enough!

Eventually our rights agreement with the BBC expired. Tom, James and I became involved in other things and the idea gradually slipped from our grasp. My copy of the screenplay has gathered a lot of dust since then, but I still think it was a good idea and that it could have worked. Perhaps others may succeed where we failed.

Ironically, the Doctor did meet the scarecrows in the end, though the Doctor turned out to be Jon Pertwee and the scarecrow was called Worzel Gummidge!

(PS I trust readers will understand that because the *Scratchman* copyright is held jointly by Tom, James and myself, I did not feel able to disclose the storyline in any detail.)

Vincent Price: he might have become the Doctor's most diabolical foe if plans for a third Doctor Who film had gone ahead

HITCH-HIKING FROM SHADA

DOUGLAS ADAMS, who was script editor of Doctor Who for two years and writer of two of its stories, has undoubtedly earned the greatest success of anyone associated with the programme. His series of four books which began with The Hitch-Hiker's Guide to the Galaxy and concluded with So Long, And Thanks For All The Fish, have sold going on for ten million copies world-wide, and recently earned him a new two book contract with an American publisher worth the amazing sum of $2.3 million! As journalist Peter Hillmore of The Observer wrote when reporting this deal, 'I expect his next book will be called something like, Hello, And Thanks For The Money!' Douglas has indeed come a long way from his impoverished youth trying to write for radio shows, and believes part of his success is due to his association with that other magical time-traveller who also goes hitch-hiking about the universe . . .

CURIOUS AS it may seem, I have to thank *Doctor Who* for *The Hitch-Hiker's Guide to the Galaxy*,' Douglas Adams explains of the book which has made him an international best-selling author. 'The idea I had behind the creation of Ford Prefect, out-of-work actor and extraterrestrial, was that he was my reaction against the Doctor.'

Douglas, who was script editor of the series from 1979 to 1980 with producer Graham Williams, continues: 'You see, the Doctor is always rushing around and saving people and planets and generally doing good works, so to speak. I thought the keynote in the character of Ford Prefect was that, given the choice between getting involved and saving the world from some disaster on one hand, and on the other going to a really good party, he'd go to the party. Every time. So that was the departure point for Ford.'

It was not until after he had left *Doctor Who* that Douglas was able to concentrate all his energies on *Hitch-Hiker* and see it develop from the original radio serial first broadcast in 1978 into a hugely popular book (plus three sequels) and then a smash-hit TV series. The basis had, though, been with him for some time, as he explains.

'The title is where it all developed and that goes back to 1971 when I was nineteen. I was hitch-hiking around Europe with a copy of *A Hitch-Hiker's Guide to Europe*. (I didn't have a copy of *Europe on $5 A Day* as I couldn't afford it!)

'Anyway, I was in Innsbruck one night, bored to tears with the place. And as I lay gazing at the stars it suddenly occurred to me that someone should write *The Hitch-Hiker's Guide to the Galaxy*. That's how it all started, and I've still got a copy of that original book. It's played quite a large part in my life, one way and another!'

Douglas Adams was born in Cambridge in 1952, and was educated at a 'reasonably good prep school' in Brentwood, Essex, which he says has 'produced ephemeral media trendies like myself, Griff Rhys-Jones and Noel Edmonds.' He has a special affection for Griff and says, 'Like Griff I'm at heart a performer – but unlike

Above: The TARDIS lands on prehistoric Earth in 'City of Death';
Below: A lazy afternoon on the Cam for the Doctor and Romana (Lalla Ward) in Douglas Adams's untelevised story 'Shada'

Griff, I'm a frustrated performer!'

Douglas's early school career was highlighted by his first rugby match at which he managed to break his nose – with his own knee! It was just the kind of crazy misfortune he was later to inflict on the Hitch-Hiker characters.

Later, he went to St John's College, Cambridge to read English and there also wrote and performed for the Cambridge Footlights Review.

This first taste of comedy writing encouraged him to try and write for a living as well as performing and directing, and for a time he was involved in stage reviews in London, Cambridge and Edinburgh.

He also, he says, had periods of acute financial need where he worked variously as a hospital porter, barn builder, bodyguard to an Arab royal family and even as a chicken shed cleaner! His already keen sense of humour was sharpened still further.

Douglas was able to contribute material to television and radio programmes – including *Weekending* – as well as working on a number of projects with Graham Chapman of the *Monty Python* team: none of which, unfortunately, came to fruition.

He also tried to interest the BBC in science-fiction without success, and during Robert Holmes's tenure as script editor of *Doctor Who* actually sent a rough draft of *Hitch-Hiker* to him.

Robert Holmes told me, 'I remember Douglas Adams sent in *The Hitch-Hiker's Guide to the Galaxy* in manuscript form and I thought he'd got talent. However, before anything emerged out of that collaboration, I'd left the show.'

This was not, however, to be Douglas's last contact with the series. 'It was a BBC producer named Simon Brett who finally took interest in my idea and got me to finish *Hitch-Hiker*. It took me six months to write the first radio series for which I was paid £1,000. I decided then that I just couldn't afford to be a writer, so when I was offered a job as a radio producer I just grabbed it.'

Six months later and Douglas Adams was offered the chance to make the transition to television – and *Doctor Who*. It was not as surprising an offer as might at first seem the case – for his predecessor as script editor, Anthony Read, had commissioned his four-part story

'The Pirate Planet' aired in September 1978. It remains to this day a piece of work of which he is fond.

'I really liked that script,' he says, 'though it would have been much better in six parts. Because it had to be cut so heavily to get it down to size, an awful lot of good stuff really went out of the window.

"The Pirate Planet" actually shouldn't have been so overtly funny or jokey as it was. I wrote it with a lot of humour in it, but the point is when you do that, it very often gets played to the hilt. I felt there was too much feeling of, "Oh, the script's got humour in it, therefore we've got to wheel out the funny voices and silly walks," which I don't think does it a service.'

This experience helped shape Douglas Adams's attitude when he took over as script editor himself. 'I think *Doctor Who* is essentially a drama show, and only secondarily amusing,' he says reflectively. 'My aim was to produce apparently bizarre situations, and then pursue the logic of them so much that they actually became real.

'You'd have somebody behaving in an interesting and apparently outrageous way. You think – at first – that it's funny, then you realise that they mean it and it's actually for real, which makes it, at least to my mind, more gripping and terrifying.

'The trouble is that one always knows that as soon as someone says, "Let's have a bit of fun with this bit," that they are going to spoil it. I can, therefore, understand people saying we weren't taking *Doctor Who* seriously – but, in fact, in the writing of it I was taking it *very* seriously.

'It's just the way you make something work – to do it for real. That's why I hate the expression "tongue-in-cheek". All that means is it's not really funny – but they still don't do it properly.'

Douglas remembers his time with *Doctor Who* as being a 'very interesting period.' He took his fair share of attacks from some hard-core fans who thought he introduced too much levity into the series.

'Certainly there were some absurd things,' he says, 'and some funny things, but there was also some excellent drama and inventive stories.'

He also particularly recalls the problems he had with the script of 'City of Death' (1979),

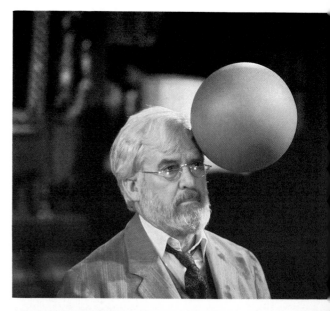

Above: Dennis Carey as Professor Chronotis in 'Shada';
Below: A bemused Tom Baker;
Opposite: A mystery for the Doctor to solve in 'Shada'

widely publicised because of the appearance of the two top comedy stars, John Cleese and Eleanor Bron as a pair of art-lovers.

'The script writer (David Agnew), who was one of our regular and reliable contributors, had

apparently been going through a terrible personal crisis. He had done his best under the circumstances, but we were in deep trouble. It was Friday, and with the director arriving to start production on Monday, we needed a new four-episode show.

'So Graham took me back to his place, locked me in his study, hosed me down with black coffee and whisky for a weekend, and there was this script. It ended up with all sorts of bizarre things in it!'

Douglas was also, of course, directly involved in one of the bizarrest episodes in the history of *Doctor Who*. He was the author of 'Shada', the six-episode story which was destined never to see the light of the TV screen because of a strike at the BBC. Or to be precise, only a tiny segment of it featuring Tom Baker and Lalla Ward on a punt on the River Cam was to be utilised when the fourth Doctor decided against appearing in the special anniversary show, 'The Five Doctors'.

Douglas has very mixed feelings about 'Shada' despite the fact it was located in the beautiful countryside of his native Cambridge, was set against the background of the kind of college life he had experienced, and was also an excellent mixture of drama and comedy. [The story-line, incidentally, has already been fully documented in my previous book, *Doctor Who: A Celebration*.]

'It really wasn't that great,' he says. 'It's only acquired a notoriety because it wasn't made. It's much more alive in people's imaginations because of that.

'It certainly had some nice bits in it, but it was widely over-long at six parts. It had a lot of padding in it.'

Tom Baker, however, does not altogether agree with this verdict. 'The "Shada" business was terribly disappointing, a great shame,' he says. 'Douglas had written a clever script and we had done some exciting filming at Cambridge. At the time we couldn't believe it was lost – they had spent so much on it and we'd done studio work and everything.

'It was also Graham Williams's last story before he left the series, so that was sad for him. Of course they couldn't even remount it when the strike was settled as the cast were doing other things.'

Tom also remembers the problems he had

learning to steer the punt on the River Cam near Emmanuel College – the name of which was changed to St Cedd's for the purpose of the story.

'I'm not much good on water,' he says, 'and all I seemed to be able to do was move the boat in every direction but the one in which we wanted to go. I even managed to get the pole jammed in the river bed on one occasion. The one time I *did* steer it correctly the cameras weren't filming!'

A feature of the story was its special effects designed by David Havard, in particular the Think Tank Globe, a sphere which floated through the air towards its intended victim. As the sphere touched the head of its target, it would then 'drain' all his or her knowledge.

An ingenious device was also created by David Havard to launch the sphere from the hand of its controller, Christopher Neame, playing the 'mind thief' Skagra. This was an electric car aerial fitted to Neame's wrist which enabled the sphere to glide into the air from his hand. This eliminated any wobble and made the finished effect look very chilling.

In fact, all the location work for 'Shada' was completed and also two of the three fortnightly studio filming blocks were in the can before the dispute brought everything to a standstill. It was a tragedy, for as Graham Williams commented while work was still taking place, '"Shada" is an epic story with something for everyone.'

When John Nathan-Turner succeeded to Graham's chair, he made strenuous efforts to save 'Shada', believing it could be screened as a special Christmas programme. He even asked Douglas Adams to cut the story back to 100 minutes of television time so that the already-shot footage could be used.

This still necessitated a further filming session to shoot the linking footage, however, and here the project foundered, for Nathan-Turner was never able to get the authority for this extra work. Sadly, therefore, the cans of film were placed in the BBC vaults and there they remain – though, as I mentioned, an extract was cleverly

The evil Pirate Captain (Bruce Purchase) and Queen Xanxia (Rosalind Lloyd) in the disguise of his nurse from Douglas Adams's 'The Pirate Planet'

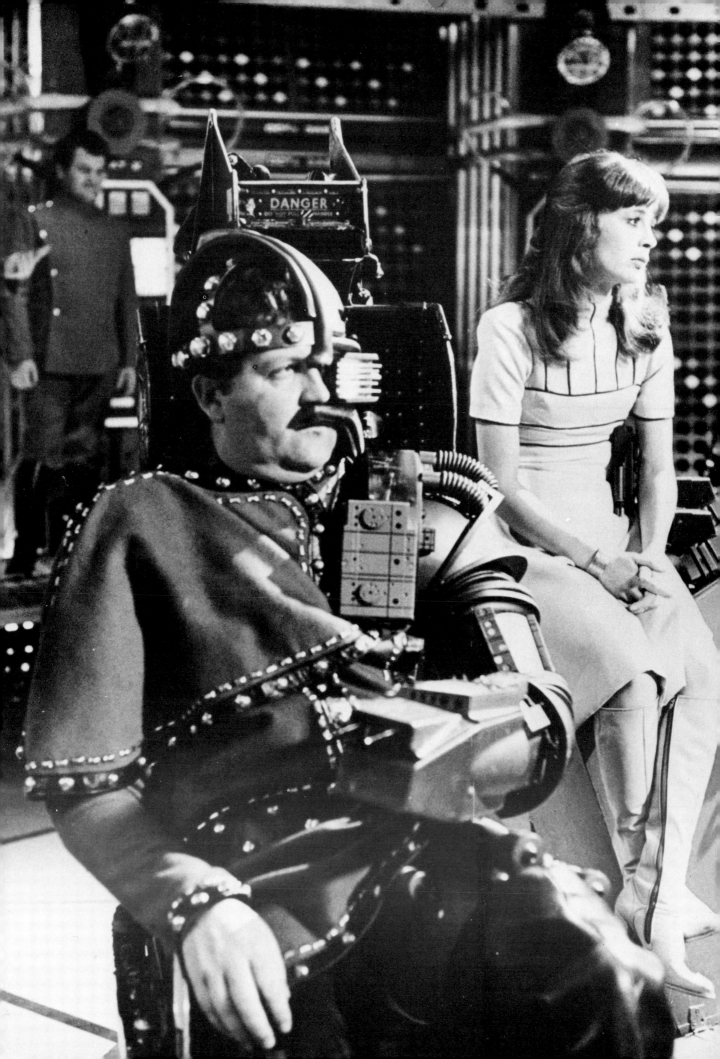

utilised for Tom Baker's 'appearance' in 'The Five Doctors'.

It was not the happiest note on which to end his association with *Doctor Who* – but enormous success with *Hitch-Hiker* lay just around the corner for Douglas Adams. And since both programmes have now become international successes, particularly in America, Douglas can see strong parallels between them.

'I think there is an overlap in the audiences,' he says. 'There are obviously a lot of people to whom *Hitch-Hiker* would appeal and *Doctor Who* wouldn't, and vice-versa, obviously.

'I believe that part of *Doctor Who*'s success in America is because it is typically English. And I find it rather ironic that since it has been taken up in America, there seems to be a certain pandering to American audiences, quite forgetting that what they'd gone for *was* its very Englishness!'

Douglas Adams undoubtedly deserves the success he has achieved with his imaginative writing, and it still surprises people to learn that he is no great lover of science fiction.

'I'm not really very keen on science fiction,' he says. 'I've got tons of SF books, largely because people keep on giving them to me. I've read about the first fifteen pages of most of them.

'It would, though, be wrong to think I have been trying to parody SF in my work. I have just used the devices and trappings of SF to talk about other things. Kurt Vonnegut did that. He started with one or two ideas he wanted to convey and happened to find some SF ideas that suited his purpose.

'Not that it's fair to compare me with Vonnegut. A much stronger influence on my writing is P. G. Wodehouse, but nobody ever notices that – because he never wrote about spaceships!'

Which comment prompts an intriguing thought. If the fates had not conspired to take Douglas Adams hitch-hiking away from *Doctor Who*, might not his sense of humour have brought a little of Bertie Wooster and Jeeves into the characters of the Doctor and his companions?

Another view of the Pirate Captain and Queen Xanxia as they use the planet Zanak to drain other worlds of their energy

THE WIZARD OF WHO

Mat Irvine *is a special effects designer at the BBC who has frequently worked on* Doctor Who *since the Tom Baker era. During these ten years he has seen and been involved in several remarkable developments in the technique and quality of the effects used in the programme. In this article he describes how the excellent visual wizardry of the present day has advanced from the early days of 'flying on a wire and a G-clamp.'*

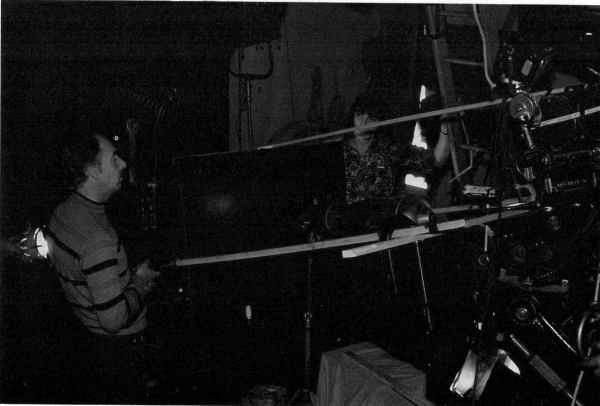

DOCTOR WHO and Special Effects have become somewhat synonymous – if only for when you admit working for the BBC Visual Effects Department and are met with a blank stare, you can at least volunteer further 'you know, *Doctor Who*, and all that . . .' Whether they like the programme or not will probably colour their reply, but at least you are usually on the right track.

I'm not sure exactly why it should be that the magic words *Doctor Who* will explain all, but I have to say that it has kept the Department busy over the last twenty-plus years, and although one could name a number of other programmes that have had an equal, if not greater Effects effort, it still comes back to the good Doctor.

Perhaps it is the feeling that they couldn't do it without us. Sometimes I think they would like to try, but to date every episode has had a Visual Effects designer more or less in control of a number of assistants, working like crazy to produce yet more miracles with not enough time, and even less money. All of us in Visual Effects have worked on *Doctor Who* at some time or other, some more than others, and I suspect we have all had our ups and downs – to quote an oft-used phrase. I know I have.

It did seem to run at a more leisurely pace 'in the old days', though on reflection this is probably because one tends to force oneself to remember the good bits only. Actually, things should have been more hectic, for whereas these days to entertain the thought of working on a *Doctor Who* without at least the back-up of the entire workshop of forty assistants, plus half a dozen contractors seems foolhardy. (In reality it is more like three or four assistants, it is just that you are constantly told by the Visual Effects job allocator that you are using the whole workshop!) But in the good old days a *Doctor Who* could just about be tackled by just one Effects Designer, working more or less on his own.

This is where I came in.

I recall that the first ever contact I had with a

Above: Ian Scoones makes adjustments to the Ogron vessel while suspended above is the smaller police ship
Below: Solving a model problem with G-clamps in 'Frontier in Space'

Doctor Who episode, besides watching it at home, was being brought down from the Visual Effects Department at the Open University to 'help out' for a couple of weeks or so. The helping turned out to be for Ian Scoones, late of Hammer and *Thunderbirds* and then the BBC. The story (I discovered later) turned out to be 'The Curse of Peladon' – quite a famous episode as episodes of *Doctor Who* go, and Ian was at that time involved with model filming.

The TARDIS had to land on a narrow ledge on the side of a cliff, and later in the story fall off that self-same ledge. However, the light on top of the TARDIS had to flash at some point in the proceedings and the problem with the model TARDIS is that it didn't – flash, that is. My first job for *Doctor Who* was to make that lamp flash!

I soon discovered when I joined the Visual Effects Department that one thing you could be sure of is that the place was cluttered with drawers and filing cabinets stuffed full of – well, useful *stuff*. The motto was 'never throw anything away' though that's long gone out of the window, for if we'd kept everything useful in the thirty years of the department's existence, we would be overflowing an area larger than the Isle of Wight by now.

But at that time things seemed somewhat simpler and there were drawers stuffed full of interesting items; items that any sensible person or organisation would have disposed of eons ago, but if one is into Effects, well, you never do know when it might come in handy.

During these searches I came across an electrical device encapsulated in a block of resin and labelled grandly on the duplicated sheet 'Metronome Unit'. Further investigation revealed it to be a circuit that would produce the audible beat of a metronome for all budding musicians. However, as a side note, it mentioned that the circuit would also, in addition to the loudspeaker, flash a low voltage lamp. In the event, the circuit never saw a loudspeaker, instead it just had to flash the lamp – and being a smallish unit it would fit inside the TARDIS model, just about by the time the batteries were crammed in. Whether the unit was designed to work just a lamp and not a loudspeaker I have no idea, all I do know is that it did work for some years on and off (which is the way most lamps flash!), and is as good an example of Effects lateral spin-offs as any I know.

From what I remember – and it was some time ago – the model filming went fine. It wasn't *Star Wars*, but then *Doctor Who* never is, and anyway this was before *Star Wars* and a lot of this we were doing first, and can we help it if they have more time and money?

The models were filmed at high-speed, which must have been my first experience of such wonders. It was more than likely to have been 35mm, and consequently an R-35 Mitchell camera; it was after all at a time when the realisation on just how much 35mm stock cost when compared with 16mm had to hit home, and anyway 35mm is so much nicer to work with . . .

For some strange reason which I've never quite been able to fathom out, the Department kept me on, but it was a little while before I encountered *Doctor Who* again. We in Visual Effects do not specialise (except, that is, for those who do specialise) so most of us move from one type of job to another. Consequently the next *Doctor Who* story turned out to be 'Frontier in Space', with a fair amount of model filming in the company of one of the two co-founders of the Department, Bernard Wilkie as Effects Designer. Ian was the main assistant, and I was trainee teaboy with a bit of gofering on the side (some of my Assistants say I still am . . .).

This time, though, it was not just the TARDIS in the story: other spaceships were due to appear – Lunar Police Ships (borrowed by the Master for the occasion) and Draconian and Ogron Vessels. Ian had made most of the models, though I discovered later he'd adapted them from a pile of old *Century 21* craft the Department had bought in – well, Effects personnel are nothing if not more adaptable than others, and I recall noting a striking resemblance between the Draconian Ship and a certain craft from *UFO* when I was viewing a repeated episode a few years later. The Police Ship was a brilliant stroke – especially as Ian had used a 100 watt light bulb as the nose. This was definitely one of those models you shouldn't drop . . . I have particular memories of this craft because during the filming schedule, it was decided that the scales between this model and the Draconian

The police ship on the Moon in 'Frontier in Space'

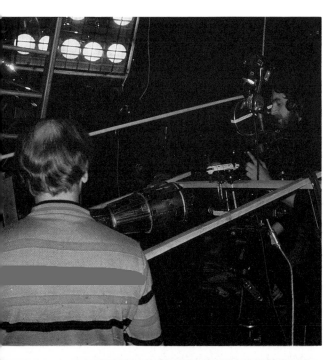

Ship, with which it was supposed to dock, were too similar. Or, to put it another way, the Police Ship was too large.

I was despatched to the workshop to make a new, similar version that would fit into the scale. It was built in a few hours – if nothing else I can work fast when necessary – and the light bulb front was matched with a ping-pong ball – which still meant you couldn't drop it!

This model film sequence was also notable for me as it ably demonstrated that things are not necessarily what they appear to be which is, after all I suppose, the whole essence of effects. Still, concerning this Police Ship and the Draconian Ship, one sequence required the latter to dock with the former. Now the latter was about 30 inches long and weighed about 10 pounds, while the former, at a stretch, probably came to no more than 4 inches and would be hard pushed to make ½ pound on the scales. Given the mass of the Draconian Ship it was far more logical to manoeuvre the smaller craft to dock with it but it had to be the other way round: remember this was before all those wonderous computer-controlled camera systems that seem to percolate all aspects of effects filming these days.

In the end, it was the smaller model that docked with the larger, though I bet no-one viewing would have realised it, for it was about one of the neatest and most ingenious solutions to an effects problem I've ever seen. The Draconian ship was attached to a substantial base and left in position – it didn't move throughout the whole proceedings. The tiny Police Ship was attached, via a short piece of rod to the camera dolly, i.e. it would move with the camera. This then meant that the camera could 'dock' with the Draconian Ship, giving a 'God's eye' view from behind the Police Ship.

This was fine as it went, but it didn't allow for the fact that the stars wouldn't move correctly. No worry, thought Bernard, they can move with the camera, but not via any computer controlled system, rather by several lengths of 2 inches × 2 inches, a larger number of G-clamps and sticky tape. The background of stars was attached to the camera dolly to move with it and hence appear stationary. In consequence, in the final picture the only object which appeared to move – the Draconian Ship – was in reality the only object *not* to have moved during the whole filming procedure.

Opposite top: Putting the final touches to the police ship;
Opposite bottom: Coming in for landing;
Above: Setting up the shot of the police ship docking with the Ogron ship;
Below: The background of stars is moved behind the miniature police ship

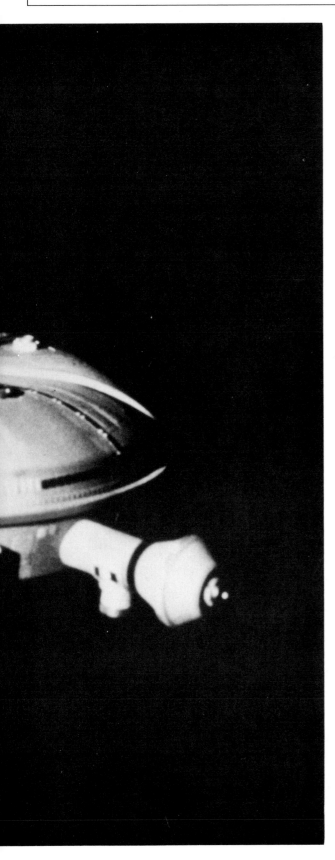

By today's standards it seems rather crude, and I suppose in reality it was, but it was a way round a problem that worked in its own way, and however technical things may appear to get these days, it's something I always bear in mind.

Things have of course, changed drastically since filming that sequence and Effects as a whole involve a far greater range of materials, skills and techniques than we had even ten years ago. Model-making uses a much wider range of materials; sculpture and prosthetics have complex foams and moulding materials to work with; while the electronics, particularly with the introduction of the microchip, have meant that making the TARDIS lamp flash in a regular pattern is as simple as the smallest circuit-board. Miniature hydraulics and pneumatics can also move effects props and models as delicately as you wish, and radio control, which used to be a daring luxury, is now used as a matter of course.

Digital effects generators can similarly manipulate the TV picture in a way not even contemplated those ten years ago, and although most of us in Effects would still prefer in many ways to work with film even this is changing. Even though the basic way a film image is exposed has not altered, the method by which it is achieved has greatly changed, and is still changing. The invention of motion control systems has taken most of the uncertainty away from using film, especially on models and miniatures, where most of the worry is about whether the movement is correct, and the depth of field of exposure is adequate.

But with all these new techniques it is wise not to forget the old. When your sophisticated radio control stops working – because you've forgotten to charge the batteries – it is comforting to remember that old method we used to use: pull it on a length of nylon line. And when the effects generator fails because someone hasn't programed the computer correctly, and you lose your electronic background – well, lying around somewhere there are usually some lengths of tape and a few G clamps!

Another model shot from 'Frontier In Space'

THE DOCTORS
SMALL AND TALL

PETER DAVISON, the fifth and youngest of the Doctors, is a cricket lover and used this to influence the appearance he adopted for the role. The stick of celery motif, however, was right against the grain because he hates the stuff! He is married to the zany actress Sandra Dickinson who suggested herself as a companion when Peter was offered the role of the Doctor! She it was, too, who played a crucial role in keeping the secret for three months when Peter became the subject of 'This Is Your Life' in March 1982. Since leaving the series, he has played a variety of roles, although he confesses to nursing one particular ambition. 'I know I'm not suave, dashing and debonaire like Clint Eastwood,' he says, 'but I'd love to be walking into the sunset with my six-gun one day!' Here, in a selection from several interviews, Peter talks about his time as the Doctor – and the special debt he owes one of his predecessors in the role . . .

PLAYING Doctor Who fulfilled all my boyhood fantasies – one of them on the very day I joined the series. The scene was not a studio set but the jam-packed BBC car park.

I was just going to my car when suddenly this unmistakable figure appeared ahead of me. It was someone who had thrilled me as a child in the very role I was now about to play, someone I had always wanted to meet.

'Congratulations,' Patrick Troughton said, his face breaking into a smile as he shook my hand. 'I'm sure you'll have a great success as the Doctor. But,' and here he paused, '*don't* stay longer than three years!'

They were words that I never forgot and I am sure, on reflection, that Pat was right. For although as an actor you live with the terror that one day there will be no work, equally you must resist the temptation to go on doing the same thing year after year.

In *Doctor Who* that temptation is very real – no matter how much fun it is and what great people you have to work with.

Patrick Troughton was also probably the most important influence on the way I played the Doctor. I wanted to include a little of all my predecessors, though as little as possible of Tom Baker because it was obviously important for my Doctor to be a complete contrast to his almost super hero figure. For myself I wanted to add elements of innocence and impetuosity.

Patrick's influence was inspired by the fact that he was the Doctor I had most watched as a kid, and I particularly admired his lighter touch. That said, I did try and make the role my own, because if I hadn't it would have been an exercise in impersonation rather than acting!

Of course taking over from Tom who had made the Doctor an international celebrity immediately threw me into a round of public appearances even before I had filmed a single scene. It was astonishing how quickly I began to get fan mail and recognition, and of course press interest was there from the very start.

I was aware of what I was letting myself in for, which is the reason why I hesitated when the current producer, John Nathan-Turner, offered me the part. I finally said yes in my agent's office late one afternoon, and it was agreed we could call a press conference to announce the fact in a couple of days.

However, no sooner had I driven home than it

The fifth Doctor (Peter Davison) is reunited with the Brigadier in 'Mawdryn Undead'

CHRIS SENIOR

ROBERT SMITH

was obvious that the story had been leaked to the press, for the phone never stopped ringing with calls from journalists.

On the *Nine O'Clock News* that night, the first story was that Ronald Reagan had been elected President of the United States – while the final story was that Tom Baker was going to regenerate into me! Friends who had been watching with the sound turned down told me later that they had assumed when my photograph was flashed up on the screen that I must have died!

What I did try to do during the three years which followed was to strike a balance. I didn't object to doing all the publicity, but I didn't want *Doctor Who* to totally take over my life. I also knew that I needed time to myself.

Whenever I did personal appearances I wasn't keen on appearing in the Doctor's outfit. I just didn't want to overdo it, because if I had I think the public would have got sick of my face!

Although people first became aware of me in that lovely show *All Creatures Great and Small*, my first real job in television in 1975 was actually not that unlike *Doctor Who*.

It was in an ITV show called *The Tomorrow People* which, as I recall, was their answer to *Doctor Who*, though it was made on an even lower budget! The episode I appeared in was very jokey and we were actually encouraged to play up the silly side. Which I suppose is the reason why it never became a serious rival to *Doctor Who*!

I have always seen *Doctor Who* as being about adventure, and one of the things that most please me about my time in the series was that we began to regularly film abroad. I believe that foreign locations inevitably add a bit more gloss to the show. I also tend to prefer location work because the sequences look visually better than those shot in the studio.

I have to admit I was never entirely happy when we were totally studio-bound. Studio work is much more concentrated because you are recording a lot of material in a very short space of time. While when you are on location you have a chance to catch your breath between sequences and think everything through that bit more thoroughly.

I particularly enjoyed filming 'Planet of Fire' on Lanzarote. The place looked absolutely great and it gave the whole story a polished look.

'The Caves of Androzani' is my favourite of all the series, though – and it was a terrific story in which to leave. I couldn't have had a better exit and Graeme Harper was a superb director. It had a pace and style about it that was quite unique and I think everybody who worked on it picked up on that.

Mind you that story very nearly killed me – literally! Running through all those sand tunnels carrying Nicola Bryant was strenuous to say the very least!

IAIN GARDNER

I had always liked the Cybermen and so 'Earthshock' is also among my favourites. It was a dynamic story with a cut and thrust that was missing from some of the other serials.

Naturally, too, I had to have a Dalek story before I left, and I would have been very sad if one hadn't been produced. The Daleks are, after all, so much a part of everybody's memories of *Doctor Who*. 'Resurrection of the Daleks' had a good, exciting script and was well served by tremendous direction from Matthew Robinson. It was also the beginning of the end for my team so it is bound to be especially nostalgic for me.

I similarly have very good memories of making the anniversary special, 'The Five Doctors', because everybody got on so well. I think there were fears to begin with that the Doctors might not get on, or that one or other would demand a better share of the action – so the script deliberately kept us apart.

In fact, quite the reverse was the case. At times during rehearsal we all naturally got a bit silly, but luckily the director, Peter Moffatt, knew when to let us enjoy a joke or bring us into line.

It hardly needs saying that I particularly enjoyed working with Patrick. He has such a tremendous sense of humour that we had a whale of a time.

It was good to be on location, too, but the bad thing was that the weather in Wales where we filmed was absolutely freezing! This time it was Anthony Ainley who was very nearly finished off when one of the special effects sequences went off with a huge explosion!

I was very sad when I left *Doctor Who* for it was certainly the biggest challenge of my career at that time. I have, though, no intention of severing my connections with the show, and I shall attend as many of the conventions as my schedule allows. As for the series itself – if there should ever be a story like 'The Five Doctors' again, then I would be delighted to come back and take part!

A. KERR

THE CASE OF
THE REPEATING DOCTORS

TERRANCE DICKS *has been associated with all but the first Doctor, as script writer and editor to the programme, as well as being the most prolific of the authors who have novelised stories for Target Books. Terrance, a former advertising copywriter turned radio and television script writer, has created several of the major elements in* Doctor Who *including the Time Lords and the Master. He is also a great fan of the programme and the way it has developed over the years of his association. 'It is true to say that it was created by the BBC,' he said recently, 'but it's one of those rare examples of a committee successfully designing a horse instead of a camel.' Terrance has become much in demand at* Doctor Who *conventions because of his unique inside knowledge of the show – although, as he says, he has no chance of developing an inflated ego when his young son makes comments like, 'I don't understand it – they're treating you like a celebrity!' In the next few pages, he talks about the curious similarities he found repeating themselves while he was writing the scripts for the two* Doctor Who *anniversary shows. But first, a little extract from his script for 'The Five Doctors' which many fans considered a 'magnificent programme.'*

THE DOCTOR: My selves ...

THE DOCTOR slumps in
their arms.

TEGAN: What does he mean?

TURLOUGH doesn't know.

TELECINE 5:

a) Ext. Eye of Orion. Day.

TURLOUGH and TEGAN
kneeling by THE DOCTOR.

He stares up at them,
blank.

TEGAN is frantic
with concern for THE
DOCTOR. TURLOUGH
although outwardly
cool, is worried and
afraid.

TEGAN: What's happening to him?
What are we going to do?

TURLOUGH: He seems
to be under some kind of psychic
attack ...

THE DOCTOR: (CALMLY AND FAINTLY)
I am being diminished, whittled
away, piece by piece. A man is the
sum of his memories you know, and
a Time Lord even more so ...

TEGAN: what can we do to
help you?

THE DOCTOR: Get me into the TARDIS
I have to ... find ... to find ...

They help THE DOCTOR
to his feet.

TURLOUGH: Find what?

IT WAS VERY much a case of history repeating itself when I was asked to write the script for 'The Five Doctors'. I had been script editor of *Doctor Who* when we celebrated the tenth anniversary with 'The Three Doctors' in 1973. Then, we had been faced with all sorts of problems to get the show on the air. But nothing like those which hit me ten years later in 1983!

It all began when I was in America in the autumn of 1982 attending a *Doctor Who* convention. It was being held in New Orleans, which is a glorious southern city which swings all night long. That night my partying had gone on until four in the morning.

Less than four hours later my sleep of exhaustion was rudely interrupted when the phone in my room suddenly rang. Blearily, I lifted the receiver and a very distant voice spoke.

'This is Eric,' the voice said.

'Eric who?' I mumbled.

'Eric Saward,' the voice replied without so much as a reference to the pun – unintended though it was. For Eric is the current occupant of my old chair as *Doctor Who* script editor.

I sat up in bed, trying to clear the fog from my head.

'We'd like you to write the twentieth anniversary special for us,' Eric went on, his voice growing in enthusiasm. 'We're going to have all the Doctors and a variety of companions and monsters. Ninety minutes long too.'

All the Doctors? I suppose I should have suspected then that it was an almost impossible brief, but the idea *did* appeal. Immediately. After all, I had been associated with the programme since the days of Patrick Troughton and this would obviously be a very prestigious show.

'I'd be very pleased to,' was all I could think to say. If I had known what was to follow I'm not sure I would have been so pleased!

Once the fog and euphoria had cleared from my mind, I came down to Earth and began to think about what I had committed myself to.

It appeared that Eric had run into the same kind of problems that Barry Letts and I had done on 'The Three Doctors.' The carefully-nurtured plans he and John Nathan-Turner had made for the twentieth anniversary had just not worked out. Now, all of a sudden, they were short of time for the show

had to go out as close as possible to the actual anniversary in November 1983. It was obviously a bit of an emergency – and there it was on my plate!

The main task I had was first to come up with a concept that included all the Doctors. Eric had forestalled any problems I might have raised about William Hartnell by telling me that they had found another actor who looked remarkably like Bill. He was Richard Hurndall who had been seen in *Blake's 7*, playing an old man uncannily like the first Doctor.

That was fine. But there were also to be various companions. The trouble there was that no-one was quite sure who of all those who had appeared would be willing *and* available!

I soon got the feeling that the programme had to be a Time Lord story, because that would be most appropriate. Then I had the bright idea of making it a kind of game.

What inspired this thought was that familiar old game where you take out a number of objects from a box and write a story around them. For wasn't this just what I was faced with – the 'box' of *Doctor Who* and the large number of objects which make it up?

This seemed to be the answer. So I started to shuffle the objects around trying to find a reason for them to fit together.

Gradually the idea evolved of somebody playing a game in which all the Doctors and their companions would be pieces on a board. Then they would be kidnapped out of space and time to provide the link.

As soon as I got that central image in my mind of a hand putting little models of the Doctors and their companions on the board, the story took on a unity that held it all together.

Initially, it was my intention to have the Master as the hand behind the Game. But as soon as I discussed this with Eric Saward he quite rightly pointed out that it would be impossible to deceive anyone that he was not the final villain.

So, instead, we chose to have the Time Lord Borusa as the villain – ostensibly trying to help the Doctor, but in fact being the Player behind the scenes.

We agreed that this was a feasible ploy, because Borusa had always been portrayed as arrogant and rather paranoid. We felt that it was possible to convince the audience that even an apparently good man like Borusa *might* become convinced he should rule the universe forever because it would be to everyone's advantage. In fact, we had to exaggerate his good points in order to make him a believable villain.

Once this concept was settled there was just the matter of introducing the various companions, as well as slipping in K9 and some of the most popular monsters such as the Cybermen, a Dalek and a Yeti.

It should have been easy from there . . .

Instead, I kept getting fresh instructions. First, they would tell me that they wanted a new element introduced – so a sequence would be rejigged to allow for it. And just when this was finished, the phone would ring again and I'd be told, 'You'll have to write so-and-so out, he can't appear!'

The Tom Baker episode was, as I said at the start, a case of history repeating itself in much the same way as had happened in 'The Three Doctors'. Then, Barry Letts and I had been unaware of how ill Bill Hartnell was until just before he was due to begin filming.

It was obvious that he would never be able to play the extensive part that had been written for him, so I had to hurriedly rewrite the script – in particular the final episode where he was due to appear with Pat and Jon in a dramatic showdown with that other renegade Time Lord, Omega.

Instead, I confined Bill to a few scenes where he would appear on the screen of the TARDIS scanner to deliver advice to his other truculent selves. Despite his illness, Bill made what I think was an impressive final appearance in *Doctor Who*.

With Tom Baker there was no health question, just his decision that he did not want to appear. I remember the sequence of events vividly.

I had, in fact, actually just completed my first draft of the script when I got another phone call from Eric.

'How's the story coming along?' he said cheerily enough. 'Have you finished?'

Proudly, I replied. 'Yes. I've just finished it.'

There was a silence down the phone and then, 'Oh, my God!'

Now to someone who knows only too well the importance of scripts being on time – and the difficulties that many writers have in meeting

PAUL DAWSON

their deadlines – this was hardly the reaction I expected.

'What's happened?' I asked hesitantly, because by now I was thoroughly used to Eric asking for changes and rewrites.

'Well,' he said after another pause, 'I'm terribly sorry, but there's been a bit of confusion between Tom, his agent and us. In spite of the fact that we thought he was going to appear, he now isn't.'

My heart fell as Eric added, 'I'm afraid you'll have to rewrite the story without Tom Baker!'

Both Eric and I knew we had to find some way of including Tom, and the idea of using some of the footage from the unscreened 'Shada' provided our solution.

There wasn't even time for me to see what had been filmed, but the footage of Tom and Romana on the river in Cambridge seemed to best fit the needs of the Time Lord's Game. So once again I rejigged the action.

In my original story, Tom Baker's Doctor was going to steal the Master's transportation device and head back to Gallifrey to unearth the plot, while Peter Davison's Doctor remained in the Death Zone and conquered the Dark Tower by the main gate.

What I devised instead was to have Tom Baker caught in a time warp making him temporarily unstable and thereby affecting the stability of his regenerated self, Peter Davison. And to show this the Davison Doctor would start fading into invisibility every now and then.

I think it gave added menace to the plot and certainly worked beautifully. I also think the footage from 'Shada' integrated so well that you would never guess that it had not been meant to be part of the story all along.

The astonishing thing is that I believe it actually improved the story, because it was easier to cope with four Doctors than five!

So there you have it – history repeating itself for the Doctor. And Who's to say (the pun *is* intended) that when the next anniversary comes around that he won't once more be playing tricks with time?

Or that I won't find myself once again back wrestling with his past and future!

And to return to Terrance Dicks' script of 'The Five Doctors', here is that unique final scene – perhaps one of the highlights of the entire series – in which the Doctor takes his leave of his various selves . . .

BRIGADIER: Goodbye Miss Smith.
Goodbye Doctor - <u>Doctors</u>.
Splendid fellows - all of you.

(HE FOLLOWS TROUGHTON
DOCTOR INTO THE
TARDIS.

THE PERTWEE DOCTOR
SHAKES HANDS)

OCTOR: Goodbye, my dear
time of my

RASSILON: And what of you, Doctor?
Do you claim Immortality too?

THE DOCTOR: No, my Lord. I ask
only that we all be returned to
our proper places in space and
time.

RASSILON: It shall be done.

THE DOCTOR: One of us is trapped.

RASSILON: I know. He too shall be
freed.

(WE SEE THE BAKER
DOCTOR IN SOME
'BACK TO NORMAL'
FAREWELL SITUATION)

So shall the one who is bound.
His sins will find their punishment
in due time.

(THE MASTER
VANISHES
LEAVING ONLY
HIS BONDS BEHIND)

It is time for your other selves
to depart. Let them make their
farewells and go. You have chosen
wisely, Doctor. Farewell!

(WITH A LOUD
THUNDERCLAP
RASSILON FADES)

THE DOCTOR: (TO HARTNELL DOCTOR)
Did you know what would happen?

HARTNELL DOCTOR: I'm sorry. I
suddenly realised what the old
proverb meant. "To lose is to
win, and he who wins shall lose."
(cont...)

DOCTOR: (cont) The whole
Rassilon's trap, to find
wanted Immortality, and
ut of the way. He
rtality was a curse, not

TOR TO HIS
LVES)

And now it seems we
odbye. I was just
now me.

CTOR: So you're the

nd the most agreeable.

OR: Certainly the

Our dress
ting any better either.

(POINTEDLY)
manners.

DOCTOR

You did quite
It's re-
y future is in
ome along, Susan.

(HE TAKES SUSAN'S
ARM AND LEADS
HER INTO THE
TARDIS)

CHRIS SENIOR

THE MULTI-COLOURED ALL-ACTION MAN

COLIN BAKER, the sixth and latest Doctor, is arguably the most energetic and certainly most colourful of the regenerations. A television star villain turned Time Lord, he has taken over the role at another crucial moment in the serial's long history. His physical and unconventional approach to the part which he had coveted for years has, though, made him the centre of controversy – some fans complaining that he is too violent and even cruel, while others have praised him for his 'impudent finesse and style.' However, one writer to the Radio Times in March 1984 declared that, 'the role of Doctor Who could almost have been tailor-made for Colin Baker.' Here we examine the actor, his career, and his personal attitudes about playing the celebrated Doctor from Gallifrey . . .

SINCE I became the sixth Doctor, many other actors have said to me, "You really are lucky – you've got the best part in the country." And do you know, it is!'

This is Colin Baker speaking after a season as Doctor Who. His handsome, curl-ringed face breaks into a smile and with a twinkle in his eyes, he adds, 'Playing the Doctor is like playing Robin Hood, William Tell and King Arthur all in one. After all, he's become a part of current mythology after twenty-one years.

'The part offers the most tremendous scope to an actor,' he says, 'and it really is in a category of its own. Hamlet talked about plays being 'tragical-comical-historical', and if you add 'scientifical' to that, then you've got *Doctor Who*!

'But it would be wrong to think the role is anything like playing Hamlet – for although each Doctor has the same name, each one is different. Indeed, you can't research a character like the Doctor, only look at the past and see what went on. That said, there isn't anything very strongly to do with the past about my Doctor!'

Studying the latest regeneration of the Doctor one can see Colin's point. The outrageous outfit is without parallel among the earlier Doctors, and only a little of William Hartnell's irascibility is discernible in his articulate, occasionally arrogant, and very witty character. Getting the part was, he says, a dream come true.

'I have been a fan of the programme since the William Hartnell and Patrick Troughton days,' he says, 'and isn't it everybody's dream to play their hero, whether it is Lancelot or Biggles or Doctor Who, because, as I said, they are all characters in modern mythology.

'I always suspected it would be good fun to play the Doctor. And I feel almost as though the part was made for me – or I was made for the part.'

In actual fact Colin nearly went after the role when he read in the newspapers in October 1980 that Tom Baker was leaving the show. He himself had been off the screen for a while after playing in the major BBC television series, *The Brothers*, in which he became a household name as Paul Merroney, 'a prototype J.R. Ewing.'

'I really got my teeth into that role in *The Brothers* and I wanted more,' he explains. 'I was hoping that they would make a spin-off series. But no offers came in.

'Then when Tom Baker finished as *Doctor Who*, I thought, "I'll ring my agent and have a go at that." But before I could do anything they announced that Peter Davison had got the job.'

When, in the summer of 1983, Peter Davison announced that *he* was about to bow out, Colin's reaction was quite different.

'This time I read that they were looking for an older Doctor, or even a woman, so the idea of going after the part didn't even cross my mind,' he says.

Fate, though, had other plans in store for him.

It all began with a phone call from the current producer, John Nathan-Turner, while Colin was in Richmond appearing in a play called *Suddenly At Home*.

'He asked me if I would come up to his office in London for a chat,' he says. 'Now, believe it or not, I genuinely didn't have a clue what it was about. I naturally asked why, but he said he would rather talk face to face.

'My first thought was that as it was summer he was going to ask me to open a fete! He gets a lot of requests like that, and I suspected he might have run out of *Doctor Who* friends who could oblige him. Also, you see, I was still getting asked to do such things because of *The Brothers* which had become a kind of cult thing – especially in places like Holland, Sweden and Israel.

'As it happened, those experiences stood me in good stead for the fame that goes with *Doctor Who*, although when I was in *The Brothers* the reactions tended to be from old ladies who threw things at me or struck me with their umbrellas!'

What, of course, John Nathan-Turner wanted to see him about was the possibility of playing the Doctor! Though nothing could be finalised then, Colin knew he would jump at the chance. Apart from being a fan from the beginning, he had also made an actual appearance in 'Arc of Infinity' (1982) playing a Gallifreyan guard named Maxil and got a feeling of the tremendous atmosphere of the show.

In fact this role had called on him to shoot Peter Davison's Doctor at the end of one episode. 'But not to get his job, though!' Colin was to joke later.

The sixth Doctor (Colin Baker) and the man who chose him for the part, Producer John Nathan-Turner

BARRY PIGGOTT

Though he did not know it at the time, this part was also the first step towards Colin being offered the Doctor's part. John Nathan-Turner explains: 'I got to know Colin during the time he played the captain of the guard for us. Then we met up again later when one of the *Doctor Who* production team got married.

'The *Who* crowd were sitting together on the grass, having a good time, and for the whole afternoon Colin kept us thoroughly entertained. Even though I wasn't actively looking for a new Doctor then, I thought that if he could hold the attention of fifteen hard-bitten showbusiness professionals for hours, then he could do the same with a television audience.'

Colin himself later recalled this day in these words: 'We were at a wedding of someone working on the series and it was one of those days in a million when you are really on form. I had no idea, though, that I had made such an impression on John.'

The week after the first meeting, Colin happened to be in Blackpool and heard something which seemed to dash his dream of playing the Doctor.

'By chance I wandered into the *Doctor Who* Exhibition in Blackpool and heard a rumour that Brian Blessed was going to play the next Doctor,' he recalls. 'As far as I know the whole thing was a rumour manufactured by the press, but it brought me up short. I have been assured since that Brian was never offered the part or even considered for it – or knew anything about it until *he* read it in the papers!'

When Colin was actually offered the part he took – he says – 'a good twelve seconds before accepting.' He did, though, borrow some old tapes of previous stories and began to assimilate the programme – though he was determined from the outset not to copy his predecessors.

The hardest thing to do once he had accepted the part was to keep it a secret until the official announcement on August 19, 1983.

'I remember we were having dinner one night,' he says, 'and this chap said to me, "My wife wants to write to the BBC and tell them you'd be perfect as the next Doctor Who. Do you think she should?" Well, I had to keep my face very straight when I replied, "No, I shouldn't think so. Knowing the BBC, they've probably already made up their minds."'

Right from the beginning Colin, who was then

TREVOR BAXENDALE

just forty years old, knew he had taken on a role that was completely different from anything he had done before in his career. Trained initially as a solicitor, he had begun acting at the age of twenty-six, and his credits included classical roles in Shakespeare's *Hamlet* and *Macbeth*, historical dramas such as *War and Peace* and TV serials including *Juliet Bravo* and *The Brothers* which, of course, earned him the reputation of being a double-dyed villain. Indeed, when it was announced he was to become the Doctor, the Scottish *Daily Record* highlighted the contrast by reporting, 'Actor Colin Baker, once a J.R.-type television screen villain, is to take on the role of one of the small screen's most loved heroes, Doctor Who!' Colin, for his part, loved the idea of being able to play the good guy for a change!

As a matter of fact, just how different the role was going to be was brought home to Colin within days of the announcement that he was to be the sixth Doctor.

'I had no idea then there were so many people so fanatical about *Doctor Who*,' he says. 'I was astonished to get my first fan letter within three days of the announcement. It was four pages long, and full of questions like, "Do you intend to visit such-and-such a planet?" and "Have you met this race of creatures yet?" and asking me about past episodes as though I should know all about them.'

He was, though, delighted to be accepted in the role even before he had been seen on the screen – especially in America which has some of the programme's most demanding fans.

'I attended the Doctor Who Convention in Chicago in February 1984 and they introduced me as Peter Davison's replacement,' he recalls, 'and after the natural reserve of the first five minutes they were very warm to me.'

Obviously an early requirement when taking over the role was to decide on a new outfit for the Doctor, and Colin is proud to say he was heavily involved in the creation of what has become known as the 'bad taste' costume!

'I spent a lot of time thinking about what I should wear, and to be honest I first thought of something not unlike the Master wears – very dark and severe. But I realised this was

A publicity shot announcing the regeneration of Peter Davison into Colin Baker. With John Nathan-Turner and Colin Baker is the Doctor's companion Peri (Nicola Bryant)

impracticable as well as unsuitable – because you can't really have two people in the same sort of costume.

'It was John's idea to have something in very bad taste, but unfortunately the designer, Pat Godfrey, kept coming up with these stunning, multi-coloured suits which were in the most extraordinarily *good* taste! We had to keep sending her away, saying the clothes were "too nice" until finally she came up with what I now wear,' Colin says.

To this suit of many colours, Colin added the unmistakable cat badge. 'Well, as Peter had utilised his love of cricket, I thought I'd employ my love of cats. The badge is intended to be symbolic,' he says, and goes on to explain: 'There is a quotation which says, "I am the cat that walks by himself and all places are the same to me." Now if you stick the word "times" in there it becomes, "I am the cat that walks by himself and all times and places are the same to me." And I think that sums up the Doctor, too, like a cat prowling through life, very contained, very sure of himself and yet capable of doing ridiculous things!'

Colin believes that there is a lot of himself in the sixth Doctor, though he has gone to considerable trouble to emphasise that the character is not an Earthman even if he looks like one, but that he comes from Gallifrey, has two hearts and even some different values.

Colin explains: 'Even though my Doctor believes in justice and truth, he is not as sentimental as Earthlings. And despite his sense of humour, love of language and other cultures, there are moments when he shows an apparent lack of concern for the people around him. A hardness just beneath the surface.'

In the light of this statement, it is not surprising that Colin has been keen to make the latest Doctor a very physical person.

'I have always felt that the Doctor must be practical and this often means taking physical action. If you are going to frighten someone into telling you something, you will probably have to make them believe you will hurt them if they don't. All the same, I never want the audience to know *quite* how I am going to act – I want to be unpredictable.

'I do enjoy the physical challenges of the role,' he goes on. 'And because we have to work

IAIN GARDNER

to a very tight schedule it is important for me to muster all my reserves of energy.'

It wasn't energy, though, that he needed to muster during an early filming sequence on location in some clay pits – but his sense of humour.

'It poured with rain, you see. Now that is all right for the film crew – they can put wellies on. But I had to walk around with plastic bags on my legs and keep wiping the mud from my shoes.'

Filming the recent story of 'The Two Doctors' did provide a physical challenge – though perhaps not quite in the way he had expected. 'During the story I had to hang on a Kirby Wire, but it wasn't the danger of falling that bothered me – but the harness they put me in.

'I'm not exactly sylph-like, and as I was hanging there, all droopy, the harness dug in and I found it very hard to breathe. I was almost gasping for breath when the shot ended!'

Colin also prefers not to use stunt men. 'I love to have a go,' he says, 'diving off things and all that. You may have guessed I am slightly mad!'

When filming another recent story, 'The Mark of the Rani' in Shropshire in 1984, he nearly tore the flesh off his hands sliding down some chains into a pit, and ran a similar risk to life and limb on a trolley.

'Some of the other actors in the show said I was mad to go downhill on that trolley. But I refused to have a stuntman because you can always tell when it is not the real person. I believe it is much more exciting for the audience to see that it is actually the Doctor in danger!'

Does taking such risks mean that Colin Baker will have a short tenure as the Doctor? Quite the reverse. 'At the moment, having waited so long for a chance to play the Doctor, I can't bear to think of anyone having played it longer than me. So that means, I suppose, I shall have to do it for longer than Tom Baker – seven years!'

And with another of those enigmatic smiles, he adds, 'I'm having a great time – and I expect to carry on doing so. It's all rather like playing cowboys and indians in real life – and getting paid for it! Whatever happens, though, the Doctor will still be the Doctor even when he's regenerated for the *seventh* time . . .'

BRIAN SULLIVAN

A LIFE OF
HAMMER AND TONGS

ROBERT HOLMES had a long association with Doctor Who which began in the Patrick Troughton era and continued right up to his untimely death in May 1986. He had written some fifteen stories spanning all the Doctors save William Hartnell, and was the programme's script editor from 1974 to 1977. His work ranged from straight adventure stories to space opera and comedy, and he was widely regarded in Whovian circles as perhaps the most popular and prolific of all the writers. Just as Terry Nation set the pattern for Doctor Who in the Sixties, so Robert Holmes helped shape the Seventies when he introduced Jon Pertwee as the third Earth-bound Doctor in 'Spearhead From Space' (1970). Because of his long association he was also the first writer invited to script the anniversary show, 'The Five Doctors' but had to decline. In this article written just before his death, Holmes offers some impressions of Doctor Who in his own humorous and inimitable style . . .

YOU ARE known,' wrote Peter Haining, the editor of this volume, 'for your feeble humour. So if you want to try to be funny about your experiences on *Doctor Who* we won't object. But do keep it down to fifteen hundred words.'

Fifteen hundred funny words! Does the man realise that four words an hour is my top limit? And that is on a good day. On a bad day, in this matter of word mileage, ancient friars illuminating religious texts in gold leaf disappear into the distance. Arthritic stonemasons chipping pious warnings on headstones – *As I am, so shall Ye be* – leave me goggling with admiration.

During one of the economic ice ages that regularly grip my household I bought a Citroen 2cv. The salesman assured me that this machine was the last word in frugality with an engine that ran on gnat's water. 'Ran', in this context, is probably the wrong word. It sort of ambled. But it was a fine car and gave one plenty of time to admire the scenery. There was also the excitement of burn-ups with passing tractors and invalid carriages.

I mention this only because it fills up some of my fifteen hundred words and also to make my point that I am the 2cv of scriptwriters.

Furthermore, not much funny happens to you when most of your life is spent in solitary confinement staring at a typewriter. Not funny-funny things, anyway. Statistically, I suppose writers must cop their fair share of ordinary funny things like train accidents and boilers going bang in the night.

I once dropped a coal-hod containing half a hundredweight of Phurnacite on my foot. As the steel rim splintered into the metatarsal that controls my big toe I remember screaming, 'Good gracious! That's funny.'

Later that day I was talking to Louis Marks, a valued though infrequent writer for *Doctor Who*. I mentioned the appalling agony I was suffering and Louis, who is a doctor, took immediate clinical control.

'Take a needle in a pair of pliers,' he advised, 'and heat it until it's incandescent. Then drive it through the toe-nail.'

Louis is one of the funniest chaps I know, as well as being a doctor of philosophy.

The aforementioned Haining also suggested I might write a few words about my last script, 'The Toe Doctors' – sorry, 'The Two Doctors'.

As a matter of fact I didn't have too much to do with this show. I did, however, attend the read-through.

This is a hallowed ceremony where everyone connected with the production assembles to meet each other and to read the script. The idea is to give the director some inkling of how long the thing will run. It also gives the costume designers a chance to talk to the actors about what they're going to wear and gives the actors a chance to talk about themselves.

'Reads', as we professionals call them, can be funny occasions. A director who hasn't done his homework can find himself introducing an ex-husband to a former wife:

'Jeremy, do you know Dorothy?'

'Of course! How are the kids, Dotty?'

'Oh, fine – now they've almost forgotten you. Incidentally, while we're on the subject, I haven't seen a penny in maintenance since last Christmas . . .'

This is known as Getting Off To A Bad Start. However, actors being actors, the chances are that they'll be the best of friends by the time the show is in the can. They might even have remarried.

Nothing like this, I hasten to say, happened on 'The Two Doctors'. On one of the hottest days of 1984 we crammed ourselves into a sudorific dog-kennel in a BBC dungeon. It was a day for sitting with one's feet in the fridge and thinking cool thoughts. I felt sorry for the actors who were due to depart for Spain. If it was like this in London they were probably already frying bulls on the pavements of Seville.

Mind you, I always feel sorry for actors. They spend a large part of their lives 'resting' (which usually means they're ferrying hamburgers about in a café on the North Circular Road) and then they have to pop up on stage and pretend to be King Henry, Parts One *and* Two. Little wonder that people throw eggs at them.

I feel even sorrier for writers, however. Particularly myself. My approach to a 'read' is to scuttle in too late to talk to anyone and hide behind the script editor. I then sit twitching like a rabbit in a room full of foxes. What will this gallimaufry of talent make of my four words an

Kevin Lindsay as Linx in the Robert Holmes story 'The Time Warrior'

hour? Surely they are already secretly hooting with derision?

Fortunately, few actors ever read the script beforehand. They arrive with their own parts underlined in fluorescent ink and with no idea what anyone else is going to say. When they laugh, therefore, in the intended places, it is as balm in Gilead to the anxious writer. It's when they laugh in the unintended places that one cringes. Actors have dirtier minds than writers and can find filth in the most innocuous lines.

Colin Baker starts it.

'Look at this pretty thing, Jamie,' he says enticingly. 'See how it swings . . . backwards and forwards, forwards and backwards . . .'

There is a ribald laugh from the cast. I glance apprehensively down the table to where Patrick Troughton is chuckling with his friend, Frazer Hines. Patrick can be funny, too. He can milk a line for its fourth *entendre*. He once explained to me that it's his way of getting all the giggles out of his system before beginning the serious acting.

I wrote Patrick out of the series and Jon Pertwee in. Now Jon's a funny chap. He doesn't use fluorescent ink but simply tears off the pages where he hasn't a line. After some episodes he would sit like Worzel Gummidge on a paper dump and wave his remaining pages between forefinger and thumb. 'A thin episode this week,' he would say.

In all my time with the programme I only got to a location twice. The first occasion was when they were filming 'The Time Warrior' somewhere near Crewe. I travelled up with Terrance Dicks, the script editor, and he's another funny chap. He ate his British Rail kippers with vinegar instead of butter, like most of us cholesterol-clogged types. He also does Yoga exercises and probably intends to live to a hundred and fifty.

Actually, I have since tried kippers *à la* Dicks and am now a confirmed vinegar man. That's all I can remember about 'The Time Warriors'.

It was shortly after this trip that Terrance told me he wanted to leave the show to devote more time to his garden gnomes. Louis Marks advised me to apply for the job. Bearing in mind the

Heironymous in 'Masque of Mandragora', written by Louis Marks and script-edited by Robert Holmes

toe-nail episode I should have laughed him to scorn. But it seemed rather a good idea at the time. Hitler probably felt the same when he sent his stormtroopers into Poland.

The lust for power gripped me and a few days later I was sitting opposite Ronnie Marsh, the then Head of Serials, across an acre of polished maple. He started telling me about the guide-lines he felt the programme should follow.

'Two or three seasons ago,' he said, 'we had some clot who wrote the most dreadful script. It had faceless policemen in it and plastic armchairs that went about swallowing people. I might tell you there were questions in the House. Mrs Whitehouse said we were turning the nation's children into bed-wetters . . .'

The thought of all that soiled linen made me put down Ronnie's awful coffee. Could it be that he was referring to 'Terror of the Autons'?

'Tut, tut,' I muttered, feeling the job slipping away. 'How awfully irresponsible.'

The BBC has a system called 'trailing' which basically means that the incomer follows the incumbent around for a few weeks. As I already knew how to read and had been a script editor before, all Terrance had to do was show me where he kept the aspirins. He went off singing merrily.

At the time I was writing some episodes of a carbolic soap opera called 'General Hospital' and one afternoon I poodled down to Elstree to see how things were going. In the control room I was introduced to various ATV luminaries, including one Philip Hinchcliffe.

'What else are you doing?' he inquired. (In television people expect you to have at least six balls in the air instead of the normal two.) I told him I'd just been appointed as the script editor of *Doctor Who* and he gave me an appraising stare. It was the sort of look Pasteur must have directed at a new microbe.

At the time I thought little of it, assuming that my face was doing funny things again. Some years ago, in a funny accident, I lost a few front teeth. After I'd stopped laughing I went to my dentist and he made me what he termed a bridge. While my bridge is nothing like the one over the Humber I am very pleased with this technological feat and my newish teeth are much better than the ones that vanished. On a sunny day I can send heliograph messages at ranges up to ten miles away.

The one problem I do have with them is that they lack sensitivity. From time to time my upper lip adheres to them and congeals in a frozen leer so that I walk around looking like Jack the Ripper surveying a home for fallen women.

The trouble is, as I'm looking the other way, I never realise this has happened until dogs and small children flee from my path. Sturdier citizens approach me truculently to ask if I need a bunch of fives.

Anyway, a few weeks later Barry Letts appeared in my office with Philip Hinchcliffe trailing him. Philip told me that at the time of our first meeting he had already agreed to produce *Doctor Who* but as his ATV contract still had several weeks to run it was not possible for him to have said anything.

Philip and I worked very well together. There is no truth in the rumour that I have bought a burial plot for him.

However, I do recall one night – it was a week-end, I guess – when I was hammering away at four words an hour to get a script into shape for the director who was joining us on the Monday. The telephone rang and it was Philip reeking of fresh-air. He'd obviously spent the day on a golf-course.

'First, the good news,' he said. 'We've got Arnold Kingfisher's script in.'

'Oh, great!' I cried. 'I knew good old Arnold wouldn't let us down.'

'Now for the bad news,' said Philip. 'It's bloody useless.'

Philip's a funny chap. He and Torquemada would have got along like brothers.

I managed only one holiday during my time as script editor. After I'd finished 'The Deadly Assassin', and with the rest of the season apparently sewn up, my wife and I slipped off for a bit of Italian sunshine.

Now this is a funny thing. We never made it.

On the *Autobahn* somewhere north of Munich the love of my life perforated a stomach ulcer. Our hilarity knew no bounds. Ankle-deep in blood, feet slipping on pedals festooned with tripe, I turned off at the next *Ausfahrt* and fetched up in a place called Pfaffenhosen which means Parson's Socks in English.

I had to hang around in Parson's Socks for three weeks while my wife was being repaired in the local *Krankenhaus*. When I returned to

Shepherds Bush there was a tangible air of crisis about the place. The irredeemable scoundrel I had engaged to write the concluding six-parter in the season had left a note on my desk. He had taken a job with Thames TV and couldn't carry out the assignment.

By that time David Maloney, the director, was practically under starter's orders. I think I wrote 'The Talons of Weng-Chiang' at rather more than four words an hour . . .

This was the only other time that I visited a location. Some of the filming was in Wapping, which, the way Philip drives, is only a minute or so from Shepherds Bush. We arrived in the gloaming and watched people from the props department spreading artificial horse dung over the road-markings. Well, I assume it was artificial. If not, Philip's car must have needed a good vacuuming.

A nice man named John Bennett was playing Weng-Chiang. While the horse muck was still being deployed a giggle of office girls, craning out of an upper window, sent down an autograph book for Tom Baker to sign. 'And can John Bennett sign it as well?' one of them called.

John raised his almond eyes skywards. 'By the soul of my sainted godfather,' he said unprintably, 'why have I just spent three-something hours in make-up!'

That's all I remember about 'The Talons of Weng-Chiang'.

I am aroused from my reverie and brought back to the present by Colin Baker. He's at it again. 'You stay here,' he says, glinting roguishly. 'I'm just going to take a scout round the back.'

He gets his laugh.

Dear God, will it never end? Sorry, God. Make that a memo to Michael Grade.

A tricky problem for the Doctor in 'Terror of the Autons', Robert Holmes's controversial story

Valentine Dyall. Considered for the part of the Doctor, he finally appeared as the Time Lord's most dangerous foe: the Black Guardian

THE MEN WHO MIGHT HAVE BEEN

LESLIE FRENCH, CYRIL CUSACK, RON MOODY, RICHARD HEARNE and *VALENTINE DYALL are just five of the best-known actors who have been considered over the years as possible 'regenerations' of the Doctor. Because of the abiding interest in this facet of the programme, I have researched the details about these men, investigated how near they came to taking on the part, and come up with the curious fact that each and every one has played a Doctor of one kind or another in their careers!*

THE ROLE OF the Doctor has been absolutely crucial to the success of *Doctor Who* during its twenty-three year history and it comes as no surprise to discover that there have been many actors considered and even short-listed for the part. Such, indeed, is the enormous popularity and public interest in the series that rumours have abounded whenever the retirement of a Doctor has been announced along with the news that a replacement is being sought.

Over the years there have, in fact, been at least five men lined up for the part who either declined the opportunity or were unable to consider the part because of other commitments – yet would undeniably have succeeded as the Doctor and certainly left an indelible mark on the character. They might even have changed the entire direction of the series. Curiously, each of these five men have played Doctors in other productions!

The first of them was the veteran character actor, Leslie French, who was actually known to the show's creator, Sydney Newman, and led the field of favourites before the first pilot show was filmed. French, who had appeared in various films (including the box office success, *The Singer, Not The Song*) as well as becoming a staple character in several of the early television serials in the late Fifties and early Sixties, was a regular in *The Avengers* which, of course, Sydney

Leslie French, favoured by Mervyn Pinfield, and a strong contender for the role of the first Doctor

Cyril Cusack, 'Ireland's greatest actor', would have brought a wealth of experience to the role of the Doctor

Newman had created at ABC Television before moving to the BBC. He had also appeared in ATV's *Probation Officer* – playing a Doctor, incidentally – and in the popular BBC series *Dixon of Dock Green*.

It could just have been this association with police boxes which made Sydney Newman think of him when casting about in 1963 for someone to play the eccentric time-traveller in his proposed series, *Doctor Who*. Leslie had also shown an aptitude for off-beat adventure stories not only in *The Avengers*, but in the late Fifties film, *The Mind Reader*.

Stories that the role of the Doctor was discussed with him and that there were plans to screen test him have never been substantiated, but there is no doubt that there were people in

the first production team who favoured him as the star – in particular Mervyn Pinfield who believed that Leslie had a wide range as an actor and an ability for more mercurial changes of temperament than William Hartnell. It was not, though, to be.

Another strongly supported candidate for the first Doctor was the remarkable actor, Cyril Cusack, who *The Guardian* newspaper recently described as 'the performer widely acknowledged to be Ireland's greatest actor'. (Though he was, in fact, born in South Africa!) Certainly, anyone who has ever met this engaging small man with his gentle eyes which can alternately sparkle with wit or malice as his parts demand, can immediately sense the unique style he would have brought to the part – probably out-Troughtoning Troughton and forever having excluded the man who became the second Doctor from his part in the making of a legend!

Cyril Cusack is the son of an Irish father and a Cockney mother – Alice Cole, a former Music Hall player and relative of the great comic, Dan Leno. He made his film debut as a child at the age of six in a film called *Knockagow* which required him to play a starving child sitting without flinching in a nettle patch while he wolfed down buttermilk and soda bread – a piece of single-minded determination which has characterised his later acting career as a master of both drama and comedy!

His whimsical and yet sometimes sinister presence in almost 50 films and countless stage and TV roles have proved him to be exactly the kind of versatile actor required to play a part like the Doctor. He is also very much an actor's actor, a man with the ability to transform his face, usually bland in repose, into a variety of responses through the merest lifting of his eyebrows or by giving a wan smile.

Of this ability, Cyril himself said recently, 'Films, TV, theatre – it's the same whatever the medium: simply a matter of projection. It's something one does unconsciously, even if the audience is invisible. I do adapt slightly, though. When I am in England I am an Irishman, but I get more easily into the English way of life than a totally Irish person would. When I am in Ireland I can be totally Irish.'

What Cyril Cusack might have done with the role of the Doctor if he had agreed to play it can be imagined from watching him in the film of Ray Bradbury's science fantasy story, *Fahrenheit 451*. Perhaps, though, with his Irish sense of superstition he would have thought the titles of two of his earlier roles were omens where any such decision was concerned. Their names? *The Doctor's Dilemma* and *The Man Who Never Was*!

Ron Moody, who played the immortal Fagin in Lionel Bart's great musical, *Oliver!* was very much the first choice as the third Doctor, according to Peter Bryant who was the show's producer from 1968 to 1969.

'Jon Pertwee wasn't my first choice for Patrick Troughton's replacement,' he revealed recently. 'That was Ron Moody. He would have been tremendous for the part. He would have brought in extra elements of comedy I felt were missing from the show at that time. I know Patrick had been cast as this kind of Chaplinesque figure at the beginning, but I think towards the end we were beginning to take the whole thing a bit too seriously.'

It only takes the swiftest consideration of Ron's career – which has earned him the reputation of being 'The Man of Many Faces' – to appreciate what a splendid Doctor he would have made. Indeed, in 1971 while he was making a film called *Mr Magic* he described his role as one that was almost a carbon-copy of Doctor Who. 'I am a mystic taking people on a tour of old-time America,' he said. 'And I use my powers to beat avalanches, wild bears, even Indians. It is all very thrilling!'

Ron may well have felt pangs of nostalgia when thinking about Peter Bryant's offer to play the Doctor – he knew that a lot of the filming had taken place at Elstree Studios, the same studios where his father had been head of the Plaster Shop and where he, himself, had first begun his working life in the Accounts Department. 'Not because I was interested in accounts,' he said. 'I was already stage-struck.'

Sneaking away to watch the film-making as often as he could, Ron later broke into the acting profession through appearing in revue sketches and entertainments and in time became – in his own words – 'a clown, a slapstick comic and the only comedian who could sing in B-flat!' (Imagine a *singing* Doctor!)

It was in 1960 that he became an international star as a result of *Oliver!* and this he followed with a number of film roles which established him as a master of character acting. Indeed, his ability at disguise reached such a pitch that while making *The Flight of the Dove* in 1971, in which he played six parts, he confessed to looking in the mirror after make-up one morning and declaring, 'I honestly didn't recognise myself!'

Ron Moody has, though, always been very much his own man, turning down many

From Fagin to Time Lord: Ron Moody was the first choice to play the third Doctor

lucrative offers abroad because he prefers to work in England. He also wishes to be known for parts other than Fagin, and one wonders if he had not declined the chance to play the Doctor whether he might not have achieved a whole new direction for his career just as the other Doctors have done.

The fourth man *Who* might have been when Jon Pertwee left had, in fact, already become an international cult figure when the offer was made in 1974 by the producer, Barry Letts. He was Richard Herne who, as 'Mr Pastry', had been the first performer to be given his own regular TV series when – according to one report – 'there were only 1,000 sets in the country'!

'Mr Pastry' in fact had become one of the most loved of all children's entertainers, a slapstick character who blundered his way through programmes for twenty years. His unmistakable trademarks of battered bowler hat, floppy moustache, wire-rimmed glasses on the end of his nose and cut-away suit, became familiar not only to British viewers, but also in France where he was called *Papa Gateau* and in Germany where he was known as *Herr Sugar Tart*. Even in America he was well-known.

It was a real triumph for a man who had been born the son of a circus acrobat and who had entered the Big Top himself as a clown at the tender age of five years old. From this beginning he developed his own mixture of slapstick comedy (he had no fewer than forty-nine different ways of falling over) which helped him break into television in the pioneer days before the Second World War. Apart from Mr Pastry, he perfected the part of an incompetent but irresistible doctor unable to carry out even the simplest examination of a patient without tripping over him or nearly choking himself on his stethoscope!

In 1970, however, at the height of his fame, Richard retired from the screen in protest at what he saw as its decline from family viewing to 'blue' entertainment. He did not want Mr Pastry to become a 'dirty old man' he said, and he would only return when standards picked up. Instead he threw himself into his favourite work of raising money for children's charities – for which he raised many thousands of pounds – and was later awarded the OBE.

It was Barry Letts who tried to coax Richard back onto the screen to play the Doctor in 1974.

Well aware of his enduring popularity as the grandfather-type character, he saw him as a complete contrast to Jon Pertwee's Doctor.

However, though Barry had no doubts about Richard Hearne's ability to play the Doctor, someone else provided a major stumbling block: Richard's *alter ego*, Mr Pastry.

Barry Letts has explained what happened. 'Richard was one of those actors who has the magic touch,' he says. 'Indeed, for years after his *Mr Pastry* series he was still opening fêtes and carnivals in the role. I invited him along for discussions about his possibly being the new Doctor, but unfortunately we established quite early on that this was impracticable as his interpretation of the part would be to play it like "Mr Pastry" – a doddery old man. And I am afraid that would not have been right for the Doctor – even in his final regeneration!'

The fifth man considered for the role was actually listed on more than one occasion – first as a possible replacement for William Hartnell and then again when Jon Pertwee left. But unlike any of the others mentioned here, he did subsequently appear in the series – though as a bitter enemy of the Doctor. He was Valentine Dyall, the famous Man in Black of BBC radio who has appeared in *Doctor Who* as the mysterious Black Guardian, and also played the part of Captain Slarn in Radio Four's recent adventure of the Doctor called 'Slipback'.

Valentine Dyall's distinctive gaunt appearance was matched by his sepulchral voice which he used to such chilling effect as the narrator of *Appointment With Fear* which ran on the radio for twelve years from 1941 to 1953. This made him a national celebrity, though he found work difficult to come by for a while after this until his career was relaunched by Spike Milligan in *The Goon Show* where he played Lord Valentine Seagoon.

The son of an actor, he became a real-life doctor after taking a degree in law at Oxford, but instead chose an acting career when a performance of his for the Oxford University Dramatic Society was praised by Sir John Geilgud. Thereafter Valentine appeared at the Old Vic, in a variety of supporting roles in the West End and in several films. 'I am,' he once said, 'the longest shining small star in the business.'

He twice played doctors on the screen – once

Richard Hearne: a possible fourth Doctor till
Mr Pastry intervened

as a Doctor Keldermans helping war-time
escapers in the 1978 BBC TV series, *The Secret
Army*, and again as a somewhat larger-than-life
character in *Who Goes Bare* – which, needless to
say, is *not* an unlisted story of *Doctor Who*!

For a time he was also associated with Peter
Cushing in several Hammer horror films – the
same Peter Cushing who played the Doctor in
the two film versions of *Doctor Who* stories
featuring the Daleks.

Although Valentine Dyall was twice on the
Doctor Who short-list, it was not until 1979 that
he was actually signed up to play the sinister
Black Guardian in the story, 'The Armageddon
Factor'. Such was his impact in the part, that
Valentine was asked to reappear in the series and
did so in 1983 in 'Mawdryn Undead',
'Terminus' and 'Enlightenment'.

The radio story, 'Slipback', written by the
current script editor, Eric Saward (and originally
called, 'The Doomsday Project'), in which he
appeared as the bad-tempered alien
hypochondriac, Captain Slarn, proved a very
poignant broadcast, for Valentine had died just a
month before the first episode of the sixty

minute story went out on 25 July 1985. It was
the very last broadcast by a man who had once
been one of radio's unmistakable voices.

Perhaps because of his gaunt appearance and
dark voice, it is hard to imagine Valentine Dyall
as the Doctor – but certainly he made a
memorable Black Guardian. I shall also
remember him for a delightful 'Who's That'
story which he frequently told with wry humour
against himself. It makes a most appropriate tale
with which to end this section about The Men
Who Might Have Been.

It concerns a man in a pub who pointed
Valentine out to his son standing beside him.

'You know who that is?' the man asked.

'No,' replied the teenager.

'It's Valentine Dyall, the Man in Black,' the
father said.

'Oh, yes,' the son answered, turning back to
his drink. 'Who's that?'

THE KEY
TO FUTURE TIMES

JOHN NATHAN-TURNER, the current producer of Doctor Who *is also the longest occupant of the job and has developed a special relationship with the programme and its world-wide army of fans (over 110 million at the last estimate). He has played a major role in promoting the development of the programme overseas since he took charge towards the end of Tom Baker's era, and is now set to re-launch the series after its break from the screen. In the following article he talks about some of the changes he has instituted, the plans for the next crucial season, and about what he calls 'The Family' of* Doctor Who, *a family of which some people have light-heartedly called him 'The Godfather'. It is in his hands and those of his team that the future of* Doctor Who *lies . . .*

JOHN SCHILTZ

and Anthony Ainley and we did a 'live' radio chat show which started just before one o'clock in the morning – and we were still there talking over two hours later! And nobody got a fee, either. That's devotion above and beyond duty in my book!

Foremost among the changes during my time as Producer have, of course, been three Doctors. I inherited Tom Baker, and have since cast Peter Davison and most recently Colin Baker. We have also had numerous companions from the team of Romana and K9 who were with Tom, culminating in a single companion, Peri. Perhaps a little insight into my thinking where the changes in companions were concerned would be of interest.

When I took over, the Doctor had a companion, Romana, who was exceedingly bright, being an acolyte Time Lord. This, combined with a computer in the form of a dog, made one begin to wonder *why* there was ever any discussion between them as to how they

AS I AM NOW the longest serving Producer of *Doctor Who* I have been involved in a lot of changes in the programme since I took over in November 1979. But perhaps foremost in my mind is the thought that, half-way through the decade, I have achieved what I set out to do: taken the show very firmly into the Eighties.

Although, of course, we have never had the budget – or the intention – to compete with *Star Wars* and similar spectaculars, at the same time there *is* a responsibility to go forward and try new, improved techniques and take a perhaps more sophisticated attitude to the show. This I think we have achieved.

It is also very satisfying the way the show has attained such popularity abroad in places like America. I particularly enjoy going there and I have have heard my role described as that of an Ambassador – which is rather flattering. It is inevitable that apart from talking to fans, I will be asked to do television, radio and press interviews and this is tremendously good promotion for the programme. Similarly, many of the actors who go also make themselves equally accessible and will put themselves out to help spread the word.

For instance, not so long ago I was in Chicago with Jon Pertwee, Lalla Ward, Janet Fielding

JNT and travelling companion at London's King's Cross Station

would solve a particular problem. One wondered why they didn't just wink at each other and say, 'We've got a 38B problem here' – and instantly put it right.

So with this in mind, a decision was taken to bring the show back to the situation where the companion represented the viewer's point of view – in other words, he or she asked the kind of questions the average younger viewers wanted to ask.

As part of this development, we went through a phase of having three companions: Adric, Tegan and Nyssa. I thought this was useful for two reasons. Firstly, because we were going into a completely new era after Tom Baker, it was important to pepper the TARDIS with new faces. And, secondly, because of the different parts the three could play: the older sister relationship that Tegan could develop with the younger ones, Nyssa and Adric.

Ultimately, though, this situation became a tremendous problem because when you have four regulars in a show such as *Doctor Who* it is awfully hard to find something for them to do. It is not like *Howard's Way* or *Dallas*, for instance, where there is always enough for everyone in the fixed setting. In *Doctor Who* you are going to a new locale for every story and each of the quartet has to be involved.

So having created characters with various dramatic attributes, how could we occupy them? For instance, we couldn't have Tegan doing just two scenes in a twenty-five minute episode and so we had to invent massive sub-plots which detracted from the main story. When you have just the Doctor and a single companion you can either split them up or keep them together depending on the demands of the story. With four of them it was a real handful and I know the writers found it incredibly difficult. Indeed, on one occasion I remember we very blatantly made Nyssa ill in the first scene of Episode One and then picked her up in the final scene of Episode Four feeling much better!

It got to be such a problem, in fact, that we had to decide to gradually ease the companions out one by one, and then went back to the days of the Seventies – Jon Pertwee's era – when there was just one companion. There's no doubt the quartet of companions worked for a while; but then the show just became too heavily loaded with regulars. Now I think it is working

LUCINDA KITZELMANN

very well again with just one companion.

During my time as Producer, a new title sequence has also been introduced, and the incidental music is often produced by the Radiophonic Workshop rather than by a single composer. And, of course, I also threatened to change the TARDIS from a police box into a completely new shape. What protests *that* brought! We did change it for one story, though, just for the fun of it!

So much has happened over the past seven years, in fact, that it is impossible to remember everything – though whenever I go to a convention there is always someone around to remind me! Occasionally, there is also a question that surprises me – though I have become more adept at handling them.

I particularly remember one concerning the TARDIS. The questioner stated that in one of

Tom Baker's stories he had said that the machine was infinite. I agreed that was so.

Yet, the fan went on, in Peter Davison's story, 'Logopolis', the Doctor jettisoned twenty-five per cent of the interior space of the TARDIS. Again, I agreed that this was true.

But how, my questioner asked, can you have twenty five per cent of infinity?

My answer was a swift, 'What is *your* name?'

The decision last year to take *Doctor Who* off the air for eighteen months was, of course, a very sad one for all of us working on the show – but the reaction of people was overwhelming and the amount of coverage we got in the press was absolutely amazing.

It was very heart-warming to know that the fans all over the world cared enough to vocalise their feelings so loudly. I understand that following the announcement on 27 February, by 2 March the BBC had received over 80,000 complaints by letter and telephone!

I do think, though, that in all the excitement nearly everybody overlooked the fact that *Doctor Who* was just one of many shows that the BBC decided to drop. And though the American fan club made this incredible and, one would have thought, highly practical, offer of £1,500,000 to keep the show going – it was *never* just a question of money. There was also the matter of BBC resources and even more importantly the availability of studio space.

There were, though, benefits from this postponement – despite the fact that some people would insist there could be none for a serial programme like *Doctor Who*. It gave Eric Saward, the Script Editor, and I a chance to really discuss and formulate the future in a calm and unhurried manner after what had been virtually a non-stop slog since 1979.

Normally Eric and I had to snatch time between studio recordings – or even in a sandpit or similar place on location – for such chats. It could be a real treadmill.

People may not realise the fact, but it takes about fourteen months to make twenty-six episodes of *Doctor Who*. So we were always commissioning the following season – and sometimes we were even writing out a companion before we had even seen them record their first story!

The postponement has, therefore, given us a breather, the thinking time to make the next season an absolutely stupendous one. Both Eric and I think it will be well worth the wait!

One of the things we are introducing is distinctly more humour. I have never liked slapstick in the programme – I much prefer wit and that will be very much in evidence. The format, too, is changing: the season will consist of a total of fourteen twenty-five minute episodes, screened one per week.

Also, the whole season will have an 'umbrella' theme – something it has not had since 'The Key To Time' series of stories. Entitled 'The Trial of a Time Lord', it will see him facing charges of intervention in the affairs of the galaxy. We shall see some of his activities in the past, some in the present, and some in the future.

Ultimately there will be a resolution – but I do want to assure you that there is *no* truth in the rumours that we are going to blow everything up at the end of the season.

The season will also see the return of Sil, the slug-like creature from the story 'Vengeance On Varos' who made such an impact on viewers. In fact, he is the first monster from *Doctor Who* since the Daleks and the Cybermen who I am told was being imitated by children in school playgrounds all over the country.

It was a shame in a way we could not bring him back immediately because of the hiatus, but I have a hunch Sil could become a major villain, a new classic to add to the Doctor's roll call of monsters.

The period off the air has also greatly strengthened my belief in what I think of as 'The Family' of *Doctor Who* – all the people who are involved in the making of the programme and the great affection they have for it. Let me give you an example.

On the day that the postponement was announced, as you can imagine the phones in the Production Office were literally jammed with people trying to get through. Among these were members of 'The Family' who were just as concerned as the rest.

Indeed, it took quite a time for some of them to get through and find out exactly what had happened. In the middle of the afternoon, Pat Troughton turned up in person at the office just to make sure that we were all right.

All around us the five lines were going mad. It

A portrait from 'Pyramids of Mars' of Elisabeth Sladen as Sarah Jane Smith

'A trim time-ship and a ship-shape team': Tegan (Janet Fielding), the Doctor, Nyssa (Sarah Sutton) and Adric (Matthew Waterhouse)

The savage the Doctor tried to tame: Louise Jameson as Leela in 'Robots of Death'

Two faces of a Time Lady: the two incarnations of Romana as played by Mary Tamm and Lalla Ward

K·9

was impossible for me and my secretary, Sarah, to answer them all – and so, do you know, Pat just pitched in and began answering himself!

He actually stayed with us for two and a half hours dealing with the press, reading out the statement we had prepared. Some of the callers must have realised who he was, but others clearly did not.

And it was most amusing when someone on the other end of the line said something that obviously made him irate, because he would quickly reply, 'Well, actually, this is Patrick Troughton and what I think is *quite* different!'

It wasn't so funny for poor Nicola Bryant, though. We had been trying to get through to her all that morning, but the line was constantly engaged.

When, finally, someone did reach her they found a very distraught young lady on the other end. She had apparently had a phone call from one of the newspapers to whom the announcement had been leaked, and a journalist had said to her, 'Would you like to comment on the fact that *Doctor Who* is dead?'

And poor Nicola assumed it was Colin Baker that had been killed!

There are lots of other stories such as those which all go to prove, I think, *Doctor Who* is one happy family – and not only those who make it, but also those who watch it, wherever they may be. And long may it continue so!

[*Editor's Note:* Shortly after this piece was written it was announced that a new companion would appear in the new season. I am sure she needs no introduction to British audiences. She is Bonnie Langford, the song and dance star who was such a success on the West End stage as Peter Pan. Bonnie will play a 21 year old computer programmer called Melanie from Pease Pottage in Sussex who is heavily into aerobics and muesli, and decides the Doctor is overweight and must diet. Apart from her natural appeal, I'm sure Bonnie will also inject into the stories some of the humour John was talking about.]

Bonnie Langford who will play Melanie, the sixth Doctor's newest companion

THE TARDIS LOG

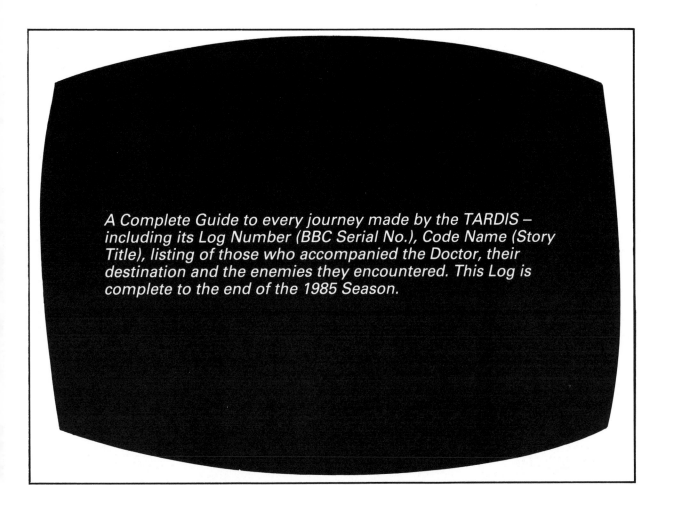

A Complete Guide to every journey made by the TARDIS –
including its Log Number (BBC Serial No.), Code Name (Story
Title), listing of those who accompanied the Doctor, their
destination and the enemies they encountered. This Log is
complete to the end of the 1985 Season.

Note:
The term 'present day' has been used for most of the UNIT stories during the Doctor's exile on Earth. There is some dispute over exactly when these stories took place, the likeliest dates being the late 1970s/early 1980s, although 'Mawdryn Undead' seems to contradict this. Similarly, the dates of many other stories set on Earth are in dispute, so wherever appropriate they have also been designated 'present day'. The TARDIS was technically grounded from stories AAA to RRR, although it did make several journeys, often as a result of the Time Lords' interference; all stories in which the TARDIS did not make a journey are indicated by a dash.

LOG NO	CODE NAME	TARDIS CREW	ARRIVAL POINTS	MAIN ENEMIES
A	An Unearthly Child	Doctor, Susan, Ian, Barbara	Earth (1963, and 200,000 BC)	The Tribe of Gum
B	The Daleks	Doctor, Susan, Ian, Barbara	Skaro	Daleks
C	Edge of Destruction	Doctor, Susan, Ian, Barbara	Vortex	—
D	Marco Polo	Doctor, Susan, Ian, Barbara	Earth (Asia, 1289)	War Lord Tegana
E	The Keys of Marinus	Doctor, Susan, Ian, Barbara	Marinus	The Voord
F	The Aztecs	Doctor, Susan, Ian, Barbara	Earth (Mexico, 1430)	Tlotoxyl, High Priest of Sacrifice
G	The Sensorites	Doctor, Susan, Ian, Barbara	Captain Maitland's ship orbiting Sense-Sphere (28th century)	Deranged Earthmen, Sensorite Administrator
H	The Reign Of Terror	Doctor, Susan, Ian, Barbara	Earth (France, 1794)	French Revolutionaries
J	Planet Of Giants	Doctor, Susan, Ian, Barbara	Earth (1960s)	Forester
K	The Dalek Invasion of Earth	Doctor, Susan, Ian, Barbara	Earth (2164)	Daleks
L	The Rescue	Doctor, Ian, Barbara	Dido (2493)	Koquillion
M	The Romans	Doctor, Ian, Barbara, Vicki	Earth (Rome, 64AD)	Slave Traders
N	The Web Planet	Doctor, Ian, Barbara, Vicki	Vortis	The Animus and its Zarbi slaves
P	The Crusaders	Doctor, Ian, Barbara, Vicki	Earth (Palestine, ca. 1191)	Saladin and the Saracens
Q	The Space Museum	Doctor, Ian, Barbara, Vicki	Xeros	Moroks
R	The Chase	Doctor, Ian, Barbara, Vicki	Aridius, Earth, Mechanus	Daleks, Mechonoids
S	The Time Meddler	Doctor, Vicki, Steven	Earth (Northumbria, 1066)	Meddling Monk
T	Galaxy Four	Doctor, Vicki, Steven	Doomed planet in Galaxy Four	Drahvins
T/A	Mission To The Unknown[1]	—	Kembel	Daleks
U	The Myth Makers	Doctor, Vicki, Steven	Earth (Asia Minor)	
V	The Dalek Masterplan	Doctor, Steven, Katarina, Sara	Kembel (4000), Earth (20th century and Ancient Egypt), Tigus	Daleks/Mavic Chen/The Meddling Monk
W	The Massacre	Doctor, Steven	Earth (France, 1572)	Catherine de Medici
Y	The Ark	Doctor, Steven, Dodo	Space Ark, Refusis (ca. 10,000,000 AD)	Monoids
X	The Celestial Toymaker	Doctor, Steven, Dodo	Celestial Toyroom	The Celestial Toymaker
Z	The Gunfighters	Doctor, Steven, Dodo	Earth (Tombstone, 1881)	Gunfighters
AA	The Savages	Doctor, Steven, Dodo	Unidentified Planet	Jano
BB	The War Machines	Doctor, Dodo	Earth (1966)	WOTAN
CC	The Smugglers	Doctor, Polly, Ben	Earth (Cornwall, 1650)	Smugglers
DD	The Tenth Planet	Doctor, Polly, Ben	Earth (South Pole, 1986)	Cybermen
EE	The Power Of The Daleks	Doctor (2), Polly, Ben	Vulcan (2020)	Daleks
FF	The Highlanders	Doctor, Polly, Ben	Earth (Scotland, 1746)	Redcoats
GG	The Underwater Menace	Doctor, Polly, Ben, Jamie	Earth (Atlantis, 1970s)	Professor Zaroff
HH	The Moonbase	Doctor, Polly, Ben, Jamie	The Moon (2070)	Cybermen
JJ	The Macra Terror	Doctor, Polly, Ben, Jamie	Earth Colony	The Macra
KK	The Faceless Ones	Doctor, Polly, Ben, Jamie	Earth (1966)	Chameleons
LL	The Evil Of The Daleks	Doctor, Jamie	Earth, Skaro (1966, 1866)	Daleks
MM	The Tomb Of The Cybermen	Doctor, Jamie, Victoria	Telos	Cybermen and Cybermats
NN	The Abominable Snowmen	Doctor, Jamie, Victoria	Earth (Tibet, 1935)	The Great Intelligence and the Yeti
OO	The Ice Warriors	Doctor, Jamie, Victoria	Earth (3000)	Ice Warriors
PP	Enemy Of The World	Doctor, Jamie, Victoria	Earth (Australia)	Salamander
QQ	The Web Of Fear	Doctor, Jamie, Victoria	Earth (Covent Garden, present day)	The Great Intelligence and the Yeti

[1]This one-episode story is included so as to give a complete list of all *Doctor Who* adventures. In actual fact, neither the TARDIS nor the Doctor appeared in this story.

RR	Fury From The Deep	Doctor, Jamie, Victoria	Earth (present day)	The Weed Creature
SS	The Wheel In Space	Doctor, Jamie	Space Station (21st Century)	Cybermen
TT	The Dominators	Doctor, Jamie, Zoe	Dulkis	Dominators and Quarks
UU	The Mind Robber	Doctor, Jamie, Zoe	Land Of Fiction	The Master Brain Computer, White Robots
VV	The Invasion	Doctor, Jamie, Zoe	Earth (present day – four years after QQ)	Cybermen, Tobias Vaughn
WW	The Krotons	Doctor, Jamie, Zoe	Planet Of The Gonds	Krotons
XX	The Seeds Of Death	Doctor, Jamie, Zoe	Earth, the Moon (21st Century)	Ice Warriors
YY	The Space Pirates	Doctor, Jamie, Zoe	Navigation Beacon Alpha 4	Caven and his Argonite Pirates
ZZ	The War Games[2]	Doctor, Jamie, Zoe	Unidentified planet, Gallifrey	The War Lord, The War Chief and their aliens
AAA	Spearhead From Space	Doctor (3), Liz[3]	Earth (present day)	Nestenes and Autons
BBB	The Silurians	Doctor, Liz	—	Silurians
CCC	The Ambassadors Of Death	Doctor, Liz	—	General Carrington
DDD	Inferno[4]	Doctor, Liz	—	'Primords'
EEE	Terror Of The Autons	Doctor, Jo	—	The Master, Autons, Nestenes
FFF	The Mind Of Evil	Doctor, Jo	—	Mind Parasite, The Master
GGG	Claws Of Axos	Doctor, Jo	Axos (time loop)	Axons/The Master
HHH	Colony In Space	Doctor, Jo	Exarius (2472)	The Master
JJJ	The Daemons	Doctor, Jo	—	Azal; the Master
KKK	The Day Of The Daleks[5]	Doctor, Jo	—	Daleks/Ogrons
MMM	The Curse of Peladon	Doctor, Jo	Peladon	Arcturus, Hepesh
LLL	The Sea Devils	Doctor, Jo	—	Sea Devils, The Master
NNN	The Mutants	Doctor, Jo	Skybase One, orbiting Solos	Marshal
OOO	The Time Monster	Doctor, Jo	Atlantis, Vortex	The Master, Kronos
RRR	The Three Doctors	Doctor (1, 2, 3) Jo	Omega's world of anti-matter	Omega
PPP	Carnival Of Monsters	Doctor, Jo	Vorg's scope on Inter Minor	Drashigs; Kalik
QQQ	Frontier In Space	Doctor, Jo	Earth cargoship (2540)	The Master/Daleks
SSS	Planet Of The Daleks	Doctor, Jo	Spiridon (2540)	Daleks
TTT	The Green Death	Doctor, Jo	Metebelis Three	BOSS/Giant Maggots
UUU	The Time Warrior	Doctor, Sarah Jane	Earth (Wessex, 12th Century)	Linx
WWW	Invasion Of The Dinosaurs	Doctor, Sarah Jane	Earth	Misguided Idealists of Operation Golden Age
XXX	Death To The Daleks	Doctor, Sarah Jane	Exxilon	Daleks
YYY	The Monster Of Peladon	Doctor, Sarah Jane	Peladon (50 years after the previous visit)	Ice Warriors
ZZZ	Planet Of The Spiders	Doctor, Sarah Jane	Earth (present day) Metebelis Three	Giant Spiders
4A	Robot	Doctor (4) Sarah Jane	Earth	Giant Robot
4C	The Ark In Space	Doctor, Sarah Jane, Harry	Space Ark Nerva	Wirrn
4B	The Sontaran Experiment[6]	Doctor, Sarah Jane, Harry	Earth	Styre
4E	Genesis Of The Daleks[7]	Doctor, Sarah Jane, Harry	Skaro	Daleks, Davros
4D	Revenge Of The Cybermen[8]	Doctor, Sarah Jane, Harry	Space Beacon Nerva	Cybermen
4F	Terror Of The Zygons	Doctor, Sarah Jane, Harry	Earth (Scotland, present day)	Zygons
4H	Planet Of Evil	Doctor, Sarah Jane	Zeta Minor (37,166)	Anti-Matter Monster
4G	Pyramids Of Mars[9]	Doctor, Sarah Jane	Earth, Mars (1911), Earth (1980)	Sutekh

[2]In an effort to escape the Time Lords the Doctor materialised the TARDIS in a succession of other places: deep space, the sea, and a jungle.

No date has ever been given for any of the stories set on Gallifrey. In the untelevised pilot episode of 'An Unearthly Child' Susan did admit that she and her grandfather came from the forty-ninth century, but this has never been mentioned on television.

[3]Strictly speaking, Liz cannot be regarded as a member of the TARDIS crew as she never entered or travelled in the TARDIS.

[4]Using only the TARDIS console, and a nuclear power source from Project Inferno, the Doctor managed to project himself, the console, and Bessie to a parallel Earth. His adventure completed he then used the console to project himself a few seconds forward in time, and a few hundred yards in space – in other words, the nearest rubbish tip!

[5]The TARDIS made no journey in this story but the Doctor and Jo did travel through time to the twenty-second century.

4J	The Android Invasion	Doctor, Sarah Jane	Oseidon, Earth (present day)	Kraals
4K	The Brain Of Morbius	Doctor, Sarah Jane	Karn	Morbius, Solon
4L	The Seeds Of Doom	Doctor, Sarah Jane	Earth (present day)	Krynoid, Harrison Chase
4M	The Masque Of Mandragora	Doctor, Sarah Jane	The Mandragora Helix, Earth (San Martino, 1478)	Mandragora Helix
4N	The Hand Of Fear	Doctor, Sarah Jane	Earth (present day); Kastria	Eldrad
4P	The Deadly Assassin	Doctor	Gallifrey	The Master
4Q	The Face Of Evil	Doctor	Unidentified Planet	Xoanon
4R	The Robots Of Death	Doctor, Leela	Sandminer	Taron Capel, Voc Robots
4S	The Talons Of Weng-Chiang	Doctor, Leela	Earth (late nineteenth century)	Magnus Greel
4U	Horror Of Fang Rock	Doctor, Leela	Earth (early 1900s)	Rutan
4T	The Invisible Enemy	Doctor, Leela	Titan, Bi-Al Foundation	Nucleus Of The Swarm
4X	Image Of The Fendahl	Doctor, Leela, K9 (Mark One)	Earth (present day)	The Fendahl
4W	The Sunmakers	Doctor, Leela, K9	Pluto	The Collector
4Y	Underworld	Doctor, Leela, K9	P7E	Oracle
4Z	The Invasion Of Time	Doctor, Leela, K9	Vardan spacecraft, Gallifrey	Sontarans, Vardans
5A	The Ribos Operation	Doctor, Romana, K9 (Mark Two)	Ribos	Graff Vynda-Ka
5B	The Pirate Planet	Doctor, Romana, K9	Zanak	Queen Xanxia
5C	The Stones Of Blood	Doctor, Romana, K9	Earth (present day)	The Ogri; Cessair
5D	The Androids Of Tara	Doctor, Romana, K9	Tara	Count Grendel
5E	The Power Of Kroll	Doctor, Romana, K9	Delta Three	Kroll
5F	The Armageddon Factor	Doctor, Romana, K9	Atrios, Zeos, The Shadow's Planet	The Black Guardian
5J	Destiny Of The Daleks	Doctor, Romana, K9	Skaro	Davros, Daleks
5H	City Of Death	Doctor, Romana, K9	Earth (Paris, present day; Italy, 1505; Atlantic Ocean, 400,000,000 BC)	Scaroth
5G	The Creature From The Pit	Doctor, Romana, K9	Chloris	Lady Adrasta
5K	Nightmare Of Eden	Doctor, Romana, K9	Empress Spaceship (2113)	The Mandrells
5L	The Horns Of Nimon	Doctor, Romana, K9	Skonnos	The Nimon
5M	Shada	Doctor, Romana, K9	Earth, Shada (present day)	Skagra
5N	The Leisure Hive	Doctor, Romana, K9	Earth, Argolis	Foamasi
5Q	Meglos	Doctor, Romana, K9	Tigella, Zolfa-Thura (present day)	Meglos/Gaztak Space Raiders
5R	Full Circle	Doctor, Romana, K9	Alzarius	The Marshmen
5P	State Of Decay	Doctor, Romana, K9, Adric	Great Vampire's Planet	Vampires
5S	Warrior's Gate	Doctor, Romana, K9, Adric	Zero Point	The Gundan
5T	The Keeper Of Traken	Doctor, Adric	Traken	The Master (Melkur)
5V	Logopolis	Doctor, Adric, Nyssa	Earth, Logopolis (present day)	The Master
5Z	Castrovalva	Doctor (5), Adric, Nyssa, Tegan	Castrovalva	The Master
5W	Four To Doomsday	Doctor, Adric, Nyssa, Tegan	Monarch's Ship (present day)	Monarch
5Y	Kinda	Doctor, Adric, Nyssa, Tegan	Deva Loka	The Mara
5X	The Visitation	Doctor, Adric, Nyssa, Tegan	Earth (1666)	Terileptils
6A	Black Orchid	Doctor, Adric, Nyssa, Tegan	Earth (1925)	George Cranleigh
6B	Earthshock	Doctor, Adric, Nyssa, Tegan	Earth, (Captain Briggs' freighter (2526); Earth orbit (65,000,000 BC)	Cybermen
6C	Time-Flight	Doctor, Nyssa, Tegan	Earth (present day, 140,000,000 BC)	The Master/Dark Xeraphin
6E	Arc Of Infinity	Doctor, Nyssa, Tegan	Gallifrey, Earth, Amsterdam, present day	Omega
6D	Snakedance	Doctor, Nyssa, Tegan	Manussa	The Mara

[6]The Doctor, Harry and Sarah used Nerva's trans-mat to beam down to Earth in this adventure. The TARDIS remained behind on Nerva.

[7]The Time Lords transported the three companions to Skaro in this story of the birth of the Daleks.

[8]The Doctor used a Gallifreyan time ring to transport himself and his friends back to Nerva which was being used as a space beacon at this time. The Time Lords sent the TARDIS back through time to meet up with the travellers at the end of the story.

[9]The Earth of 1980 in this adventure was, in fact, a projection of how the world would be if the Doctor and Sarah Jane had not defeated Sutekh.

6F	Mawdryn Undead	Doctor, Nyssa, Tegan	Earth, Mawdryn's Spacecraft (1977–1983)	Mawdryn, Turlough, Black Guardian
6G	Terminus	Doctor, Nyssa, Tegan, Turlough	Terminus	Turlough, the Vanir
6H	Enlightenment	Doctor, Tegan, Turlough	Striker's and Wrack's Ships	Turlough and Wrack
6J	The King's Demons	Doctor, Tegan, Turlough	Earth (1215)	The Master
6K	The Five Doctors	Doctor (1, 2, 3 and 5) Tegan, Turlough, Susan	Eye Of Orion, Earth, Gallifrey	Borusa; Cybermen; Dalek; Yeti; The Master
6L	Warriors Of The Deep	Doctor, Tegan, Turlough	Earth (2084)	Sea Devils and Silurians
6M	The Awakening	Doctor, Tegan, Turlough	Earth, (Little Hodcombe – present day)	The Malus
6N	Frontios	Doctor, Tegan, Turlough	Frontios	The Gravis and Tractators
6P	Resurrection Of The Daleks	Doctor, Tegan, Turlough	Earth (present day), Prison Ship	Daleks, Davros
6Q	Planet Of Fire	Doctor, Turlough	Earth, Lanzarote (present day), Sarn	The Master
6R	The Caves Of Androzani	Doctor, Peri	Androzani Minor	Sharaz Jek
6S	The Twin Dilemma	Doctor (6), Peri	Titan Three, Joconda	Mestor
6T	Attack Of The Cybermen	Doctor, Peri	Earth, Telos (1985)	Cybermen
6V	Vengeance On Varos	Doctor, Peri	Earth, (23rd Century)	Sil
6X	The Mark Of The Rani	Doctor, Peri	Earth (19th century)	The Rani, the Master
6W	The Two Doctors	Doctor (2, 6), Peri	Dastari's Research Station, Earth (Seville, present day)	Chessene, Shockeye; the Santarans
6Y	Timelash	Doctor, Peri	Karfel, Earth (Scotland, 1888)	The Borad
6Z	Revelation Of The Daleks	Doctor, Peri	Necros	Davros, Daleks

"...wait don't tell me..

never forget a face . . ."

LETTERS

Write to: Letters Editor, Radio Times, 35 Marylebone High Street, London W1M 4AA

Doctor Who: can we stand the suspense?

THE NEWS THAT THE BBC has decided to suspend production of *Doctor Who* is not merely disappointing – it is alarming. I was about to put pen to paper in praise of the present series, back in its Saturday slot at long last, very effectively extended to 45 minutes, and boasting both a first-rate new Doctor and excellent scripts. Now I discover that further espisodes are to be held up for at least 18 months. Cash may indeed be short, but where is the BBC's loyalty to the audience that has been so faithful to the series for over 21 years? . . .

Do *Who* is a unique show and it c   nds a massive following at hom   huge overseas audience,   ways it is the flagship of the Br

If this dec   n is an attempt by stealth to abandon the series altogether, then it is a quite reprehensible betrayal of audience loyalty . . .

M. S. Ball
Birkenhead, Merseyside

WHAT AM I GOING TO DO FOR THE NEXT EIGHTEEN MONTHS? THEY ALL THINK I'M TYPECAST

HAMLET REJECTION

OLIVER TWIST REJEC

Ian Dicks

No Who, no fee

. . . I am not prepared to pay a higher licence fee if the Doctor is to be suspended – perhaps permanently. If he goes, my TV goes. Alternatively, Michael Grade could go. Perhaps we should slap him into a Tardis – the Master's, of course!

Theresa Croshaw
Nuneaton, Warwickshire

Is it true?

Can it be true? The Master has regenerated and is calling himself Michael Grade.

Adrian Cale
Finedon, Northamptonshire

MICHAEL GRADE, Controller, BBC1, replies:
The response of Doctor Who enthusiasts is bordering on the hysterical given the exact nature of the BBC's decision. Doctor Who has not been cancelled, just delayed for a year. The ratings for the current series have been disappointing and we need time to consider the reasons for this. The current series is an experimental 45 minutes length and this has not proved as popular as we had hoped. We were looking to make some financial savings in the coming year and it seems that after 21 years a short rest would do the Doctor no harm at all.

Long-running television series do get tired and it is because we want another 21 years of Doctor Who that we have prescribed a good rest.

An alternative for patients

David Henshaw's *Brass Tacks – Patient's Dilemma* (27 February BB(

welcome from the new headmaster which was displayed on the notice board (BACK PAGES 16-22 February).

This letter has reinforced my fears of a fall in the standard of education as a result of the merger. Not only is the second sentence of the second paragraph very clumsily constructed, but Mr C. J. Humphries, a Cambridge graduate, uses the words 'Mrs McClusky and myself' as the subject of a verb in the final paragraph. I feel sure that Mrs McClusky would never have been guilty of such careless English.

Anne Cooper
(an anxious parent)
Greystones, Co Wicklow, Ireland

What's happened to the Howards' house?

Many thanks to BBC2 for *Forty Minutes – Whose House is it Anyway?* (28 February). No doubt Barnsley Council has been patient over the years in trying to get the Howard brothers to surrender their land but would it really hurt them to wait a little longer? There is plenty of land suitable for sponsored housing development in Barnsley without upsetting old men who ask for nothing more than to spend their remaining years on their own property.

Mr Gordon Howard is indeed a very brave man and I feel very upset th   someone of his age should h   give up what is   Howard

CELE TOY

DWBULLETIN
THE MONTHLY NEWS-'Z

Mr G

A message to   from the World's 110 mi   DOCTOR WHO Fans;

THE 100TH DOCTOR W
INTRODUCING ...

DOCTO
WH

FIRST EDITION

ROBE
Gra

We W   the D

What the papers say

Rough stuff out as the Time Lord is told to play for laughs

BY LOUISE COURT

IN the decidedly ungalactic surroundings of a Stone Age village in Hampshire, Dr Who made his long-awaited return this week.

Last year the return saw the threat of spending the rest of eternity confined to a BBC library shelf following Beeb boss Michael Grade's criticism that the show had become tired and needed a rest.

But following the fanatical response of Dr Who devotees

There will, however, be changes following Grade's warning that he would be watching the show very closely. Violence will be toned down and humour played up.

"It is going to be a touch of the Harry-poon-antics rather than Dirty Baker," said one sixth Dr Who, Colin Baker.

No one is happier to be back in front of the cameras than Baker, who had completed just one series before the show's future hung in the balance.

And the trial of the show in general is paralleled in his on-screen life of the sixth Dr Who, who is charged with meddling in the affairs of time, intervening in the course of others' lives in the course of...

At Butser Hill, near Petersfield, Hampshire, there plete replica of an Iron Age Village, with the same shattering coincidence, the DR WHO team di of OB for the first story of Seaso Amazing! They invited the pr April 10, and they ran on Saturday 12..

TONIC FOR DR WHO . .

★ DR Who is back fighting for his screen life. Zap goes the violence and in comes the rapier wit. Colin Baker said: "From now on I shall use wit instead of Dirty Harry tactics to solve my confrontations."

The Doctor was pulled off our screens for a year because the show was "too tired and too violent. New writers are giving the points a tonic for the new series, tellingly called *Dr Who On Trial*. During it the Doctor's companion, Peri—played by Nicola Bryant—will vanish forever, to be replaced by Bonnie Langford.

LAST TRIP: Colin and Nicola.

JACK BELL

Number 100

DISTURBED BY THE TIME TRAVEL EXPERIMENTS OF THE EVIL DASTARI AND CHESSENE, THE TIME LORDS SEND THE SECOND DOCTOR AND JAMIE TO INVESTIGATE, ARRIVING ON A STATION IN DEEP SPACE, THEY ARE ATTACKED BY A SHOCK FORCE OF SONTARANS AND THE DR IS LEFT FOR DEAD. ACROSS THE GULFS OF TIME AND SPACE, THE SIXTH DOCTOR DISCOVERS THAT HIS FORMER INCARNATION IS VERY MUCH ALIVE. TOGETHER WITH PERI AND JAMIE HE MUST RESCUE HIS OTHER SELF BEFORE THE PLANS OF DASTARI AND CHESSENE REACH THEIR DEADLY AND SHOCKING CONCLUSION...

HARDBACK: AUGUST, PAPERBACK: DECEMBER.

December is an historic date for Target, the paperback section of W.H.Allen & Co., as it will see the publication of the 100th novel in 'paperback' of their popular DOCTOR WHO range. The book, written by Robert Holmes, is Season 22's THE TWO DOCTORS, which will actually be available initially in hardback from August. To celebrate, DWB is giving away the full, uncorrected proof of the book. All you have to do is guess the editor's 'ten' favourite book covers—the person who sends is most correct, by July 1st, wins !

Chuckle with Dr Who

DR WHO is preparing to return to the TV screens with an injection of humour.

Violence is out, following Mary Whitehouse's complaints about the series.

Ratings soared in the last series when Mrs Whitehouse intervened. Five million viewers watched the next three episodes.

A new series is being filmed at a reconstructed Iron Age village.

It stars Colin Baker, with Nicola Bryant as his assistant Teri, in an intergalactic courtroom drama set in Britain after the holocaust.

OXO ad woman Linda Bellingham is The Inquisitor.

Filming begins this week in Petersfield, Hampshire, and it will be screened in the autumn.

Nicola Bryant will be replaced by Bonnie Langford later in the series.

Dr Who clincher for space girl Peri

DR WHO star Colin Baker gets to grips with gorgeous side-kick Nicola Bryant, as they start filming a new series of the TV thriller—called The Mysterious Planet—in Trading Surrey.

Nicola plays his part for her last series. She's making her last appearance in the space hall of fame!

Picture by PETER SIMPSON

LAUGHING: Colin Baker and co-star Nicola Bryant

Bryant and Baker: She bows out, he bounces back

Daily
, *Daily Record*,
, Today, *The Sun*,
   The Mail ran a picture
   an Sims, and *The Star*, strange-
   , ignored the story...

   rit
programi
can more
though m
Corporati
pects of
ising oper
a hefty ro
ce. The j
whole indus
to proporti
seemed unbe
"Doctor Who" nad become the epitome of a successful programme.

It is understood that after the viewing ratings for part two of VENGEANCE ON VAROS were

BBC tv

BRITISH BROADCASTING CORPORATION
TELEVISION CENTRE WOOD LANE LONDON W12 7RJ
TELEPHONE 01-743 8000 TELEX: 265781
TELEGRAMS AND CABLES: TELECASTS LONDON TELEX

MORE DOCTOR WHO IN 1986
ANOTHER MIRACULOUS ESCAPE FOR FICTION FAVOURITE

As every follower of 'Doctor Who' knows...You can't kill a TimeLord.
Today Bill Cotton Managing Director of BBC Television phoned David
Saunders, co-ordinator of the 'Doctor Who' Appreciation Society, to
explain the BBC plans.

He said: "'Doctor Who' will be on the air in 1986, as it is in 1985,
and as it has been for each of the past 22 years."

"Instead of running in January 1986 we shall wait until the start
of the ~~~umn schedule, and then 'Doctor Who' will be a strong item
in th~

~ld tradition and have 25
~rsion running at the
~ does the

~ we need to
~lso means that
~ greater number

~ support of the fan

MYSTERIOUS SEASON

Season 23 is still shrouded in a veil of mystery, particularly with regard to
what differences there will be between it and its predecessor. John Nathan-
Turner was unwilling to elaborate further on the increased humour content that
the press reported on when Bonnie Langford was announced as the new companion,
except to say that there will not be any slapstick.   The show, itself, now seems
to face a similar dilemma over violence to the one it faced in 1977 when Graham
Williams found himself with no alternative but to tone down that element and
replace it with humour.

But all is not a complete mystery.   The structure of the season has now been
confirmed as 4 - 4 - 6 and the opening four part story by Robert Holmes has been
assigned the working title of THE MYSTERIOUS PLANET.   Various production staff
to be involved on this one have now been named in addition to director, Nick
Mallett.   The Designer is John Anderson, who provided the scenic designs in
RESURRECTION OF THE DALEKS, while the Costume Designer is Ken Trew, whose first
credit was for TERROR OF THE AUTONS and who, more recently, designed the colourful outfits seen in SNAKEDANCE.   The Make-up Supervisor will be Denise Baron,
who was responsible for THE TWIN DILEMMA.   Finally, Visual Effects will be in
the charge of Mike Kelt, who worked on ENLIGHTENMENT and designed the latest
TARDIS Console first seen in THE FIVE DOCTORS.   THE MYSTERIOUS PLANET or whatever it ends up being called will see a week's location filming at the beginning
of April followed by two studio sessions at the end of April and in early May.

Nicola Bryant will bid farewell to "Doctor Who" halfway through the season, and
if you take this literally, it would mean that Peri departs during the third
episode of the second story, which will now definitely not be called PLANET OF
SIL.   As with all three stories this season, there will be some location
filming.

Is the third and final story (now confirmed as a six parter) which is
~ounded by most mystery.   This is the story in which Melanie is first
~ted to appear and therefore a location shoot in Pease Pottage seems likely.
~s "Doctor Who Magazine" is still reporting that Robert Holmes is writing
~rt story for Season 23.   Is this incorrect?   Or does it mean, in rests
~hat a great deal of responsibility for the future of "Doctor Who"
~ of this veteran scripter?   Or, as has been speculated elsewhere,
~irected by a hawk or a dove?   Will it be an Earthbound tale?
~with Christopher Hamilton Bidmead?   No doubt, all these questions and more will
~pers have reported?
~r the coming months.

~, John Nathan-Turner still says he believes that "Doctor Who"
~nd Season 23.

~ISON ~

~ctor Who is probably one ~
~ as when it starts there ~
~' months. With this in mi~
~eason 23 COUNTDOWN mont~
~late and re-cap to keep ~

~ill continue to see~
~ng title sequence ~
~ the same: at one ~

~r are provision~
~, 7B Planet of~
~urse Robert H~
~isode order~

~o note is~
~takes pla~
~rture...W~

~rs sc f~
~ord si~
~g she~
~g thr~

~n s~
~to~
~i~

~'T let
die !'

of a DOCTOR WHO
~es. In 1986 it was...
~urteen

~ISTICS
~wspaper,
~reporting
~lished a
~ inside
~hat the next
~HO would
~isodes—half
~aker's last
~third the
~of episodes
~on by William
~ck Troughton.
~rned the speakers
~ations. "Do the
~of the general
~ve high priests
~oration would lower
~o confiding their
~plans to oafs as
~Sun' journalists?"
~gist of another Press
Release ~astily issued t o
stave off a further tidal wave
of "hysteria" from the fans.
And it worked. The Duty Office
phones remained quiet, the mail
bags stayed at low volume, and
even 'The Sun' abandoned its
interest in the story, preferring
the blue tits of the '85 English
summer to the bum steers of
disgruntled BBC employees...
Only two people outside TV
Centre's sixth floor appreciated

(Cont'd Page 6, Col'1...)

And with ~
on 'The ~
promise of ~
ublic face ~
~ce proudly ~
~ 85 minute ~
~eries pr a ~
~ weeks". ~
~e one man ~
~s 6th floor ~
~TOR WHO , ~
~r patience ~
~octor back ~
~adding as ~
~ident that ~
~eat future ~

PanoptiCon 6 Speci

~RESS—Death of 'Who(Page

Dr WHODUNIT

BEEB

WHILE the BBC is firing Dr Who into a time-warp, the Tories are blasting ahead with their own twisted version of the programme.

They are presenting a long-running series in which the Mad Monetarists, who are far more monstrous than the Cybermen or Zygons, always triumph at the expense of the poor, sick, disabled, unemployed and elderly.

It is useless trying to adjust your sets or switching off. This horrific story is for real.

Further rise

The latest episode Chancellor Nigel Lawso ing the National Health aided by Social Service ary Norman Fowler Dalek cries of "Exte Exterminate!"

Because of Mr Lawson' spending limits, a furthe prescription charges loo likely.

If, as some experts are f ing, the cost per item

from £1.60 to £2, it will be TEN TIMES what it was when Labour left office in 1979. Mrs Thatcher denied then that she was planning any increase at all.

This would not be quite so bad if the money saved was spent in preventing any further cutbacks in hospital services, to shorten the waiting list for life-saving operations.

But more and more hospitals are being forced to turn patients away, even though doctors know that many of them will probably die before they reach the head of the queue.

At Guy's Hospital in London, for example, the magnificent heart unit faces closure for four months because the surgeons have overspent their budget by £272,000. Their crime? They carried out more operations than originally planned

the Chancellor cannot pas~ much in

Shocks and changes for millions of TV fan

Dr Who down-Gra

And a new look at Crossroads

Daily Mail 28.8.85

BBC C

SWITCH

HIM O

18 M

DOCTOR time lock Michael was furi

Actor Lord, appoin take mon

hi tr

Unmasked

For 22 years, to the delight of millions of viewers the world over, Dr Who has with wholesome aplomb survived the worst that time and space could hurl at him.

Now—supposedly for reasons of financial economy—he is to be vaporised off our screens for more than a year.

Even the BBC could not of its own voltion do so dastardly and a deed. No, there i explanation

HOLD TIGHT! Dr Who—Colin Baker—taking new partner Melanie—Bonnie Langford—on a gala

y, he ects. But ma t to get the incr

.0. said: 'I'm astounded it to axe its most popular pro duct. If I were an ordinary member of the public I would express my rage.

'The programme is part of

gry BI

ewers

gin

WAR OV

DR WHO

AS GRAI

PLANS

SCI-SER

he Daleks failed BBC 1 Controller M cceeded. He had beaten Dr Who ... o ed until yesterday.

ade's decision to cancel the good doctor's next he £2 million for other projects upset thousa

ed to the cause and thus w chapter in the amaz Time Lord. It is like itself.

read on .. he scene : Mr Grade is slithering about on the ps, while at home the Who bandwagon has ling.

By PAUL DONOVAN

Who fans are conscious Grade's decision to post as until by P mined e on tl

prove terminal for the eternal voyager.

The BBC something in

Funny that ers was sa With on giant industry.

't is not very a woman w power to know she sit in bed eat

nd partially sighted, opens at the Natu ames Ditton, Surrey, explored a deer w ot to grips with a dolphin. The exhibition ru

BBC enters a time warp

By Stephen Cook

The controller of BBC1, Mr Michael Grade, may well be longing by this morning to step into the Tardis and whisk himself beyond the range of the outcry stirred up by his decision yesterday to postpone the next series of Dr Who.

Work on the new series, originally scheduled for January next year and starring Colin Baker and Nicola Bryant, was due to start in a month's time.

But Mr Grade has decided that the money would be better spent on other drama projects and that the Doctor must be shelved until the autumn of 1986.

The Dr Who Appreciation Society, mouthpiece for the 110 million watchers in ntries, is furious. Mr Haining, author of a en Dr Who's 22-year his- r V the move was dis- Over horrifying and

Colin Baker — a delayed return to screen

"What other programme could change the central actor and his character and still hold a magic grip over each new generation?" he asked. "Dr Who is unique. There will be a tremendous outcry to save it."

Mr Haining recalled that Mr Grade's last controversial decision — to interrupt the current run of Dallas so as to spoil commercial television's plans

for the next run of the soap opera — had been reversed by a public outcry, and he predicted a repeat performance.

The BBC denied that the decision was a ploy to persuade the Government that it does need a £65 licence fee in order to give the public what it wants.

"Dr Who almost certainly does earn far more through sales than it costs to make, bu it has to be made out of th drama budget, and sales into the BBC's general coffer The drama budget this yea was not big enough to everything," a spokesman sai

A decision to switch Dr Wh from Saturday to mid-wee was reversed by public pref sure last year, but a campaig failed in 1980 to save the do tor's dog, K9—despite suppo from the World Wildlife Fun

Last night the managing d ector of BBC TV, Mr B Cotton, said he was sorry abo the postponement but the BBC had to live within its incom

if the more implicit these

Frank special

more over

urney d and

the int is er to ustice actory ment.

Clubs try to save Dr Who

Fans of *Dr Who* were yesterday attempting to save their hero - and were even considering offering the BBC a co-production deal to stop the programme from being discontinued for 18 months.

American fans suggested financial backing to save the next *Dr Who* series after news of the BBC decision reached the United States.

"Organizers of *Dr Who* fan clubs were so shocked they stayed up all night to start 'Save the Doctor' campaigns", Mr Ron Katz, a spokesman for one of the American clubs, said.

He said there were 100,000 members in official clubs in the United States but there were milion more fans throughout the country.

Insid that D licenc view misj BBC Doctor. Colin Ba Gr to the series, Da probably have th of other people. J. good financial off.

has ra T Nor is the BBC team delirious at the losing one of its mos money-spinners. In i Dr Who has be 54 countries.

Was it so smart to p programme which not only a big audienc much-needed income? with the answers is G is on holiday, mulling latest audience resear shows that while th planned EastEnders audience of 17.35m on Tuesday - only 1m ITV's Coronation Stre own innovation, the weekly Wogan, did no the top ten.

Short of cash

FUTURE DR WHO

THERE was good ne Who fans yesterda Grade controller c pledged to ru nthe 21 years after its su His recent announce shelve the series ca roar among devotee 'Long-running TV ser get tired, and it is l we want another 21 y Dr Who that we hav scribed a good rest, Grade writes in the issue of the Radio Times.

es, of co an re early re ar re on tl itself.

s ty. the doctor's long term fear the 18-month lay-off ma

SHOCK FOR DR. WHO

DOCTOR WHO is being time-warped off the air to save cash.

The cult show—the BBC's top selling programme overseas—will take a year's rest.

BBC1 chief Michael Grade has swung the axe so money can be poured into new programmes.

Last night a disappointed Colin Baker, who plays the Doctor, said it was a "terrible shame." And he warned the lay-off could be "dangerous."

He said: "If there is any intention of getting rid of the show, it will be much harder after a year off the air for people who care about the show to effective op...

"I think it is the end of one of the traditions killed off."

The which Saturda next m —makin longes Britis

By PAT CODD

And it is at its highest spot in the ratings for five years, with nearly eight million viewers.

Doctor Who has achieved cult status in the United States and Colin Baker reckons the BBC should try to sell it even harder there.

Pledged

TV favou... given yea... in cash...

galore!

DAILY MIRROR, Thursday, Febru...

SEE THE NEXT WE...

Dr Who dropped in new cuts by BBC's timelord

TA-TA RDIS!

...years, met his match yester... day in the Amazing axeman— BBC-1's new controller Michael Grade.

Grade has already despatched beauty contests, Superstars and the World's Strongest Man.

Now he has ordered Dr. Who—Colin Baker—his assistant Peri—Nicola Bryanth to take a "rest" once their current adventures in the tardis time machine end next month. The decision, to save cash

...to make other dramas, shocked both stars.

Nicola said: "It's like being poleaxed. I'm just back from America where 4,000 Dr. Who fans screamed in ecstasy and said: 'You're wonderful.'"

The pair, who were to start a new series in May, are not due back on screen until Autumn 1986.

But furious fans began bombarding the BBC with complaints last night.

DR WHO: Baker

BBC cash curbs ground Dr Who

By HARVEY LEE Television Staff

DR WHO'S flying telephone kiosk was grounded yesterday for 18 months by the BBC, which says it cannot afford the £100,000 cost of each 50-minute episode of the Time Lord's adventures.

When the present series ends next month, the Tardis will not materialise again before autumn next year — the longest break in its 22-year galactic wanderings.

Filming of the next adventures had been due to begin this spring.

But the BBC's money problems threaten to achieve what the Daleks never did...

Peter Who!

BONNIE FLIES TO RESCUE OF TIME LORD

PETER PAN has been called in to try to save Dr Who's life.

As the Time Lord's new assistant Melanie, 21-year-old Bonnie... the West End's Peter Pan, will in... ject humour in place of the violence which upset BBC-1 boss Michael Grade and threatened to finish off the 22-year-old TV space saga.

Melanie, a modern miss heavily into aerobics and muesli decides the doctor is overweight and must diet. The current Dr Who, actor Colin Baker, is about 15 stone.

Some "stunning" new monsters and the return of Sil, the galactic slug are promised in the series starting in the autumn.

Money Worries?

MAKEP... Glynis

...y, Peter Davison and Colin Baker

...y, Alan Grisbrook, Brendan Beirne, David Thorpe, Gar...

ON 24 1985

...ool and we will be ad... ng it as a major tourist ...ction," he said.

...is hoped to keep the site ...for at least three years. ...e rest of it has been sched... Gardens.

Mr Donald Forster, chairm... of the corporation, promised development.

...Britain are said to be... Gadafy.

Student organisations last night said that they were ing to see if the recalled ans were Gadafy support ing back for a pep tal... cross-section, some of... might be in danger.

No reprieve for the Doctor

By Stephen Cook

BBC TV has decided to stick to its decision to postpone the next series of Dr Who from January until Sptember next year despite protests from the programme's followers.

The managing director of BBC TV, Mr Bill Cotton, yesterday telephoned the Dr Who appreciation society and said he recognised the "passionate support" of the fans in Brit-

ain and abroad but wanted them to be patient.

The programme would be screened next year, as in each of the last 22 years and the 1986 series would be longer than at present because the episodes would be 45 minutes rather than 25.

A BBC spokesman added that Dr Who repeats from the programme's early years might be shown in the season beginning in autumn.

Peter Fiddick... Enders, the BBC's... opera, was launche... dience rivalling long-running targe... onation Street. The first... sode was watched by 17.35 million people, just one million fewer than saw the Lancashire saga, and enough to make the newcomer the number four show in last week's ratings charts.

Leader comment, page 14

---

only home produced science-fiction programme shown by the BBC, as well as being an immensely popular programme with all ages.

Is Mr Grade planning some sort of blackmail? Does he think that by cutting back popular programmes he will force the licence money up?

He's already failed with the Dallas fiasco — perhaps he'll realise the British public won't be pushed around. Who is the BBC run for, anyway?

SUSAN FLOWER, Chesham, Buckinghamshire.

... Not only is Dr Who one of the most popular drama programmes, it also earns the BBC considerable sums overseas because it is exported to more than 50 countries.

Is this yet another Michael Grade decision designed to upset viewers, following the Dallas proposals?

The BBC should go ahead with their original plans to screen Dr Who. And if they wish to save money, they ought to sack Mr Grade.

COLIN WILSON, Bicester, Oxford.

Dr Who and Peri: high grade series.

Dog tired

MRS J. D. COOMBS [Letters] should visit Marple if she believes 90 per cent of fouled pavements are caused by loose dogs turned out by unthinking owners.

When stickers were dis-

played recently on lamp-... warning of a £50 fine, n... dog-owners went round... ing them down, and al... their animals to use the... posts!

At the school where I t... we have to check and... children's shoes. Mothers...

FIVERS

"Give us the freedom to decide if we want fluoride in our water supply."

BBC1 controller

"Doctor, we're prescribing a rest."

NAM...
ADDRES...

PETER ANG...
25 Woodvill...
Sale, Cheshire.

Causes of dec...

From Mr Peter K...
Sir, In your...
27) Dr...
asto...